Molly and the Muslim Stick

David Dabydeen

MACMILLAN
CARIBBEAN

Macmillan Education
Between Towns Road, Oxford, OX4 3PP
A division of Macmillan Publishers Limited
Companies and representatives throughout the world

www.macmillan-caribbean.com

ISBN: 978-0-230-02870-8

Text © David Dabydeen 2008
Design and illustration © Macmillan Publishers Limited 2008

Typeset by EXPO Holdings
Cover design by John Barker
Cover illustration by Derek Walcott

Printed and bound in Hong Kong

2012 2011 2010 2009 2008
10 9 8 7 6 5 4 3 2 1

MOLLY AND THE MUSLIM STICK

"England leans heavily upon, and against, Islam – its ancient and recent encounter with Islam – for its sense of nationhood."

Joseph Burgundy

"Middle-Eastern sticks do have a habit of metamorphosing: talking, turning into snakes, splitting the sea and, now, taking over novels. What has always intrigued me about the Moses story is why the snake returns to being a staff when Moses tries to hold its tail: is it shy? or is the 'will' of the staff awakened by Moses' touch? Or is the lesson: try to hold the tail/tale of anything and it vanishes?"

Hisham Matar

"In the nightmare of the New World of Guiana, which was Raleigh's dream of El Dorado (they executed him not for the absence of pure gold but for the nightmare prospect of debased metal), all mingle and cross-fertilise, bud and flower into forms that are mongrel in sex, race, religion. The English rid themselves of Raleigh as mongrel bud and counterfeit coinage."

Elizabeth Knowles

DEDICATION

For Robin Dabydeen, brave and dearest.

ACKNOWLEDGMENTS

Thanks to Marjorie Davies, Erin Somerville, Lynne Macedo, Jonathan Morley and Michael Mitchell for making this novel possible by their typing and comments on various drafts, and to Derek Walcott for creating a special painting for its front cover. Especially to Rachel, for her extraordinary patience and constant encouragement.

PART 1

Once upon a time – the night of Wednesday 26th October 1933, when I was fifteen – it happened. It. It. The dripping down my thighs. Sticky, then thickening to treacle. As bloody as flesh from Leviticus. I lay awake listening to my bleeding, above the hog-snoring of my father who rested beside me. An hour before I had tried to shut out the moonlight which was as ubiquitous as dust. It was a full moon but more incandescent than I had ever seen it, sending out a light of such strength that there were no shadows in the street, nowhere for a rat or insect to lurk. The street was silent, for such was the eeriness of light that people stayed indoors in fright. It was as if there had been some accident in the sky and an enormous continuous spillage of white paint. The light poured into the house with the force of a breached dam. It swirled around spots of dirt on the shelf, on the bed-frame, on the door handle, magnifying them so that they seemed like boulders in rapids, threatening havoc and the shredding of life. I closed the curtains but the light bore through them, fanning out throughout the room. Dad came home, banging the front door to signal his drunkenness and frustration. I had covered my face with a blanket, but he peeled it back, exposing me to his want. I struggled when he lifted my night-shirt, but then I surrendered, imitating Mum in her quiescent state. The light was relentless, making me witness all his doings, the unbuckling of his belt, the placing of his mouth on my nipple, the bunching of his fingers at my thighs. There was a moment of huge pain, then convulsions and tremors, and throughout it all explosions of light, flashes of insight. The beatings didn't start then, but when they did, stars were born in my eyes.

The next hour I washed away my blood, sticky, resinous, and awaited the morning when I would clean the house with devotion, and tend to Mum as if nothing new had happened that night. I cooked and served him breakfast. He ate hungrily, focusing on his belly, not the slightest evidence of guilt as he stuck his fork into a plate of sausages. He left the house, returning late at night to be with me. At first he would claim me in a drunken mood, but after a while he came to me in a normal frame of mind. I preferred this matter-of-fact approach, for afterwards he would snuggle his head under my fledgling breasts, like a rat or insect seeking shelter in a clean space, away from its normal habitation.

Even the beatings I came to accept. I was pre-destined to endure them. The Bible spoke of Jesus stumbling under the weight of the Cross and the heaviness of Pharisee hands. The first blow was anticipated. I was sitting at the table selecting a passage from the Acts of the Apostles to read to Mum. The night before Dad had approached me but it was a strange visitation, for instead of the usual hard insistence, the forced entrance that seemed to hurt him as much as it did me, he lay beside my body and whimpered. I reached out to comfort him but he would not be touched. He just lay there whimpering, then his pitch changed, becoming a whine as fearful as the siren's that went off when there was a pit accident. He stopped abruptly and began to flutter and words issued from his mouth that were garbled and mutilated as if he was possessed and speaking in tongues.

No, Dad whacking me on the head was not an unexpected act. He was pecking at me, wanting to draw blood because of his crying the previous night, the panic that had seized him, the need to keep distant from me. I had reached out to comfort him but he had withdrawn and bayed in distress. After the blow I continued flicking through the Bible, searching for verses to share with Mum. Confused by my lack of response to his violence he slapped the Bible out of my hand and stormed out of house. The Bible fell to the floor, opening up at a passage from John, which I read to Mum. It told of the risen Christ refusing Mary's embrace, denying her gratitude for His survival. I read the verses to Mum uncaringly, for my mind was twinkling with remembrance of the blow from my father. I looked upon the pages dancing with stars, and thought of Mum scouring the night sky for some sign that our life was more than a scramble for a sliver of meat. I wanted to reassure her of the truth of romance, the truth of her vision of Accrington's courtly and refined past, which could still be resurrected, but even as I read aloud from the Bible my words were drowned out by the noise of the thud on my head and the noise of a bird craving the protection of its mother.

*

Once upon a time I was a child of eight or nine playing by myself in an alleyway with pieces of coal, pretending that some lumps were oranges, others pears, and I was a greengrocer's assistant, weighing and parcelling fruit for customers, collecting their money and giving them correct change. "Ooh, let me have that one back," I said to an old lady, taking a pear from her basket. "It's a bit spongey underneath, your eyes are too gone to notice the patch. Here, let me give you a fresh one. Or, seeing you're old and poor and bent-backed you can keep it for free, just don't tell that stingy Mr Mean Grocer or I'll get the sack." My chattering to the old woman was suddenly interrupted by a squawking in the tree at the mouth of the alleyway. I went up to the tree and discovered a fledgling bird crumpled on the ground, scraping its wings in the dirt in an attempt to fly. Its mother was calling out from the tree from which it had fallen. A black cat appeared from nowhere, a ragged thing that snarled as it approached. The bird fluttered and let loose a series of cries so loud for its tiny frame that I was afraid its throat would burst. The coal in my hand became a granny-smith apple, hard as stone, which I hurled at the cat. It yelped as the apple landed on its skull, collapsed and seemed to die. I cupped the bird in my hand. Ssh, ssh, ssh. I whispered soothing words to it but it did not want to be touched. It squawked even louder, a mournful plea not to be killed. In its desperation for life it pecked and pecked at my fingers, drawing blood. I hugged the tree and hoisted myself up using my arms and legs, keeping the bird secure in my hands. I deposited it in the nearest branch, slipped to the ground and watched from afar as its mother swooped down to be with it. When I reached home my mother beat me for tearing and bloodying my dress, scrubbing me hard to get rid of the resin which leaked from the tree and smeared my skin. I didn't mind, nor did I weep, for what was my punishment compared to the terror that had afflicted the little bird? And what was it all for, the shrieking of the innocent bird, the growling, then the yelping, of the innocent cat, and who was I, the child in their midst, with sorrow for the bird and a spiteful applestone for the cat which travelled through the air and stopped at its skull? Stone. Air. Skull. Death. Why?

*

I was nearly thirty before I broke free from my father, going away from Accrington to the Leeds Institute to train to become a teacher of English. Up till then I stayed at home cleaning. Cleaning from the time my mother sickened. Cleaning the kitchen, the hallway, the stairs, the daily deposits of colliery dust, and the bath – especially the bath, our family being among the privileged few who owned a modern one. My father had bought it brand new with the earnings from my mother's clairvoyance business. A huge deep enamel thing, which our neighbours used to marvel at when my father allowed them in to bathe. In 1940, when a flotilla of sailing boats set off for Dunkirk, they said, "Oi, Norman, if you put to sea you could rescue half the bloody British army in one of these." And my father beamed in pride at the bright vessel in the house. When my mother died a year later he no longer cared for it, choosing to wash in the back garden with bucket and tin cup. It was I who cleaned it every day, to keep alive the memory of my mother. Polishing, I was always polishing, first her crystal ball, then, when she was laid out, I polished her eyes so that the neighbours could see in their sheen evidence of her gift of prophecy. Death and burial, but the polishing didn't end, for there was my nemesis, the bath. It had been acquired under questionable circumstances, and when I rubbed it with a white cloth I was wiping away her sins, preparing her soul for the safety of heaven, far away from her lies (were they lies or occasional flashes of insight?), the colliery grime (real enough and regular), the mills' cacophony, the blare of Salvation Army trumpets at the end of the street, drunken wagoners spilling their loads clatteringly on the pavements, the rapture and rowdiness of football crowds… the experiences of my childhood abbreviated for Terence's delectation, Terence the gentle boy from the elegance of Graston, a leafy Kent village. Accrington, my home town – he liked the name, the hurtfulness of it. It was like eating grit and cracking your teeth. Axe. Crud. Rind. Arid. Acrid. Acid. Cringe. Terence would chew upon the harshness of my upbringing, savouring my hurt. Afterwards he would polish my body with his tongue until I felt comely and sylvan, the memory of the war years erased for a while, the night-time sirens, the factory discharges, the screaming of the burnt.

One day, driven by hunger, my mother and I set off to forage the woods for mushrooms. It was 1941, the time of war rations. I was in my early twenties. She wore a green frock patterned with red flowers which were still visible despite the years of washing. I wore a maidenly white cotton dress which belonged to her (it was the left-over pieces of cloth with which I used to shine the bath for years afterwards). She was in a gay mood, weaving her arms into mine, hatching plans to re-settle elsewhere after the war.

"Fed up with Accrington and its slate tiles falling off rooftops," she said breaking away from me, stooping and scouring the undergrowth. "Sweet Molly, let's go where it's green and wide-skied. I've always wanted to give up the dead folk business and milk cows instead for a liv–". I seem to remember her face brightening with a smile as if she had discovered something more unexpected, more valuable than toadstools. Then the sun was gouged from the sky and my eyes were sealed in darkness.

At the inquest they said she had disturbed an unexploded bomb nestled in the undergrowth, dropped there from some previous air-raid. The shell went off at the touch of her hand. She took the full blast but though the rest of her body was tattered flesh, her face remained intact, serene. I was thrown at a distance and lightly injured. The local newspaper, desensitised by war casualties, poked fun at her: "Accrington medium fails to foresee her death. Daughter Molly blinded by blast." (I was blinded but only for a day, my sight returning suddenly).

*

War had framed my mother's existence. The Second World War killed her but the first one gave clairvoyancy. It was 1918, and I was two months lodged in her womb when the siren went off signalling a pit disaster. "It's bad this time, Maureen," a neighbour said. She had brought a gift of an apple as a way of compensating my mother. "And to think your Norman only got taken on last year. As luck will have it he'll be one of the gonners. Should have stayed in his window-cleaning job, your Norman. More money down pit was it? It's the war, pits are flat out producing coal. And money's good if you can get it. He'll be a gonner now, poor

Norman, should have stayed safely up his ladder." The neighbour gabbled on indiscreetly, even after my mother had fainted.

Norman arrived home a few minutes later, perfectly intact. It had been a false alarm and in any case he was shovelling coal above ground that day. He sped home to reassure his bride. He found the neighbour crouched over a prostrate Maureen. An elderly woman, she was a veteran of countless siren calls, and herself widowed in a mining accident. She worked her teeth steadily to the apple core. When my mother came round she reached to touch my father's face, hesitantly, for it was as pale as the face of the deceased. She reached to touch the agitated ghost of her husband and incipient father of her child. She found warm flesh, wet with the sweat of worry. She fainted again. The neighbour picked her teeth, swallowed the fragments of apple and left.

My father feared that the shock would cause her to miscarry, but I was snug in her womb and my mother recovered swiftly. She was transformed though, as anyone would be who had touched the face of a ghost between bouts of fainting. It started at the kitchen sink. She was washing a cup when she suddenly let it fall and stepped back in surprise. "It's Mark Garnett's cup, that," she said, her words laden with fright.

"Who's Mark?" my father asked.

"I don't know. Only had a glimpse of him. He was raising the cup to his lips. It had black tea in it and two spoonfuls of white sugar." She plucked up courage, took a plate and rubbed it with the dishcloth. "This belonged to Caroline Collins. She was an old woman with grey hair curling from her chin and no teeth. Her favourite food was black pudding because she could mash it with her fork and suck on it." All our crockery was second-hand, so my father let her be. He put it down to her banging her head when she collapsed at the feet of our neighbour. She would come right soon. In any case, he had heard somewhere that pregnant women had odd thoughts, odd yearnings.

My mother spent the rest of the war months of 1918 identifying strangers in the house. She wandered about with a cloth in her hand, wiping things to reveal their origins. The windows, she said, were put in by one Joseph Countryman. A skilled carpenter, he made the frames himself. And the door. And the kitchen cupboard with its black doorknob. It used to be gleaming white but age had fouled it. The iron sink was made from left-over scraps which a blacksmith had crafted from hundreds of worn-out horseshoes. She didn't know his proper name. Everyone called him Smithy, or sometimes Blackie. She seemed to see everything in black and white, my father noted. Which is why, to cure her of the malady of single vision, he bought her a green dress adorned with red floral designs, and brand new so that she could wear it for the first time when she gave birth to me. Brand new, but the expenditure was worthwhile, even on his small wages, because then she would stop prattling about the past, take up the baby and begin life afresh.

November 1918. The war ended. I was born. The demand for coal fell. My father was laid off. We lived on scraps. The clairvoyance didn't cease, for the blanket I slept under was, according to my mother, a donation from the Salvation Army. It once belonged to a cat called Leah who lived in a mansion in Leeds, the owner being a cloth manufacturer. The blanket lined Leah's basket. It was especially woven, but its white threads quickly darkened, giving it a cheap dingy appearance. On the cat's birthday it was replaced with a new garment. The blanket, twenty years old, passed through several alms-houses until it reached me as a rag. My father listened in despair. The food dwindled in the cupboard (made by Joseph Countryman, the carpenter: every time she went to the cupboard more of his biography was revealed. He was a solitary man, more in love with the tools of his trade than with the prospect of a wife. He died in 1899. Hanged himself. Only twenty-seven, poor thing.

And such a moon-white face lying in his coffin! When you hang yourself your skin colour changes, all the blood in your face leaks out of your mouth, she said. There were dark rumours about his relationship with the boy apprentices he took on…). My father resorted to pawning his belongings and it was on one of his last visits to the pawnshop that he noticed, among the bric-a-brac, a crystal ball. He took it instead of cash. And that is how my mother became famous in Accrington. Instead of wandering around the house identifying the biography of wood, brick and iron, she would sit in one place and gaze into glass. And the stories she told were simple, straightforward, black and white. The ball became the teats of a cash-cow, and because of my father's flash of cunning in the pawn-shop, and my mother's mental condition, the fortunes of our family changed dramatically.

Black and white stories. Tales told to the living of the dead. The war had left hundreds of widows in our town. My father calculated that notices put in shop windows advertising his wife's clairvoyance would bring them in in droves. And they came, the numbers of bereaved swelled by pit accidents and of course natural deaths. From the time of my birth and throughout the 1920s our house was host to folk – mostly women – seeking news of those crushed under machinery, drowned in mud, blown to high-heaven by enemy guns. Consider the following as a typical scene in the drama of life and afterlife. A winter's day, wind howling outside, curtains drawn to shut out the cold and the remains of the sun, the parlour sombre but for the dance of candlelight and flames flaring lustily in the grate. My mother sits at a table on which is set her crystal ball. The table is austerely white and bears no pattern to disturb the mood of the event. At the other end of the table are three tense widows. My mother makes them link hands, to show shared sorrow. My father stands behind them, his face stiff as an undertaker's. Sandalwood burns above the fireplace but the scent is spoiled somewhat by coal-dust in the air. My mother places her palm over the crown of the crystal ball, rubs it, closes her eyes, moans. One widow breaks out in an involuntary sigh. Grief salivates on their faces. My mother continues to rub and moan, the women's agitation increases. Suddenly my mother opens her eyes and stares at them, commanding silence. She bends her head to the ball, almost touching it with her mouth. The glass is frosted over by her breathing, and it is through this haze that she stares before speaking.

Mum (she is wearing a black linen dress with a white collar and white edgings at the sleeve): "It's Robert then, is it? Robert's the name, eh?"

The three women (two are unadorned but a third, in spite of her condition of widowhood, wears pink studded cloth earrings, and her mouth is smeared in pink lipstick, as if she had just been roughly kissed) stare uncomprehendingly at my mother.

Mum: "Well, if it's not Robert, it's Dave then. Is it Dave?"

Silence. The widows looked confused. Their hands begin to part. My father looks down at the women, but particularly at the pink one with breasts all too visible in her low-cut dress.

Mum (in a voice more exasperated than desperate. She lifts her head to address them): "Robert, Dave, Ernie, Charlie, there's a throng of them. Most of the limbs are torn off, and so much bleeding together you can't tell one from the other."

The women break hands. The first presses hers to her mouth to stifle a sob. The second stares out into space in a state of shock. Only the pink one speaks: "He's dead is he? Our Harry is dead?"

Mum: "Harry… now let me see. Harry…" She scries until she eventually locates him. "Yes, to tell truth your Harry is shot so full of lead he weighs half a ton sunk in the mud."

"Are you sure? Sure it's our Harry?"

"Sure as niggers live in Timbuktoo I'm sure. He's so heavy with lead the stretcher-bearers can't lift him, so they leave him to rot where he lies."

The first woman can no longer contain herself. She lets out a grievous croak. The second fans herself to maintain consciousness. Only Mrs Pink is unimpressed by the mud of the battlefield. She leans towards the crystal glass to get a better view, her breasts straining at her top in excitement.

The pink one: "They told me he's missing in action but for years I've been expecting him to re-appear any day."

Mum: "He'll not come back, not for the likes of you, you can count on it, unless his skeleton can rattle its way to the beach, row across the channel and hitch a lift from Dover to Accrington."

"Can Harry speak? Can you make him speak to me so I'll know he's dead?"

Mum: "Can't, love. Dunno how to, I've only just started this business, not tuned my voice yet to theirs on the other side. I can only see him. Come back in a few months time, I should have got the skill by then."

Mrs Pink's chest heaves with disappointment and my father looks on sympathetically.

Mum: "Wait! Wait! Someone's writing in the mud."

First widow: "Who, our Mike?"

Second widow: "Is it Johnny? He was a fine one with a pen, a dozen letters from the front he sent me. Love letters they were, sweet and all…" She begins to cry.

Mum: "Hush, woman, let me concentrate. It's not Johnny, it's Harry. He's taken up his gun and writing with the tip of the bayonet. A-R-F-U-R." Mum looks accusingly at Mrs Pink. "Makes sense to you? A-R-F-U-R?"

Mrs Pink is so taken aback she has to cough to get her breath out. She rises weakly from her chair. My father steps forward to support her, putting his arm around her waist and walking her to the door. She is unsteady on her feet like a bride walking down the isle, the wedding ceremony done. Mum watches her struggle to maintain balance in her high-heeled shoes. Mum watches Dad's arm wrapped just below her bosom. The other two women follow them out, confused, tearful.

Dad (returning from seeing them out, first having taken a shilling from each. He is of stern aspect but makes an effort to control his anger): "Maureen, do you have to be so hard on them? They're still tender you know, from their loss."

Mum (clearing the table of the white table-cloth and the crystal-ball, turning her back to him): "Hard? How do you mean hard?"

Dad (sinking his hand into his pocket to feel the shillings): "Do you have to talk about guts spilled out or heads cracked open, all that nasty war stuff, can't you just say that they've passed over or something?"

Mum (turning around to confront him, her face trembling with accusation): "Hard? It's that woman who's hard, not me!"

Dad (confused): "I only meant—"

Mum (enraged, shouting): "A right slut. War's not even over and she takes up with a man called Arthur. Poor Harry, he can't spell, neither this side of life nor the other. Some people never change but his steadfastness is better compared to that loose bitch."

Dad (contrite. He says nothing. He remembers squeezing Mrs Pink's flesh, consolingly. Her body gave off a sweaty perfume. He looks down to the floor to conceal his emotion. After a while he takes the money from his pocket, clears his throat): "Not bad for an hour's work, what do you think, Maureen? Let's drink a beer to celebrate."

Mum has turned away from him again, but she can still see the shillings and the silver longing in his eyes.

*

Mum could see everything from the time she woke up from her fainting, but her new gift only darkened her outlook on life. She used to think her marriage to Norman promised, if not a magical transformation in their lives, at least a chance to leave Accrington, its pits, cotton mills, dyeing units and cloth printing shops. In Accrington she would end up as a factory worker but she dreamt of life in the smokeless south, where she could train as a typist and stenographer, gaining a respectable career as a secretary in a City firm. Norman was barely literate compared to her – she had showed a natural aptitude in school for reading and composition – but he was a hard-worker, shovelling coal as if born for such activity in spite of his slender frame. During the war the pits boomed, his wages were just sufficient for a little saving. After the war they would migrate away from the grime to a green place, buying a house overlooking one of many London parks and commons, or perhaps settle in a leafy village. Norman would work as a labourer, and their joint wages would give them a comfortable life, eating in restaurants, taking holidays on the south coast. The children, when they came, would sleep under white sheets, warm new blankets and be pampered with toys.

Now she saw Norman for what he was, common and mean-spirited. She remembered the day of their marriage in 1917 when Norman cried poverty. Instead of a grand celebration in the Town Hall, with piano and violin, he booked a space in the local pub for a dozen people. Cheese sandwiches, and being 6 o'clock on a Saturday, the trumpets and bassoons of the Salvation Army on the street corner serenading them with 'Onward Christian Soldiers': Norman had timed the wedding party to coincide with the appearance of the Salvation Army, so as not to pay for musical entertainment. At the time she was too proud of her new status as a bride to bother with the paltriness of the surroundings. And her parents, drunk on ale, kept complimenting her on her dress, her beauty, her good fortune. She'd never seen them so effusive before. They were taciturn and dour but the wedding had loosened the constraints of their nature and they babbled and slopped alcohol upon the table. She never suspected that their delight was in ridding her from their home, Norman now responsible for her bedding, her food and clothing. She looked adoringly at Norman, amazed at her bounty. It was scarce a year since their first meeting in the church hall, when the neighbourhood had gathered together to hear the latest news of the war. The vicar announced the disaster: hundreds of Accrington men feared dead at the Battle of the Somme, mowed down by German machine guns. Valiant men all, loyal to King and Country, now safely in the bosom of our Lord. "What greater love than to lay down his life…" The platitudes flowed over the heads of the shocked gathering. My mother didn't harbour resentment against the vicar: it was his job to try to make sense of the slaughter. My mother was simply angry at the news. She remembered a few years back the jubilation in the town when war was announced. There were queues of men outside the Town Hall volunteering to enlist. The war, she knew, meant the prospect of adventure, of journeying away from mill and pit to foreign parts where a moment of heroism could make your fortune, see your name emblazoned across the *Accrington Observer*. She was understanding of them, even excited for them, for what was she, what were her parents, but nobodies? Her father had never voyaged abroad. The furthest he went into foreign and dangerous territory was the quarter mile from the surface to the innards of the coal mine.

Now, as the vicar spoke, she was angry. She broke the hush of disbelief by standing up and addressing the vicar. It was the first time she had questioned authority, but her voice was surprisingly bold for one so young. "Exactly how many have been killed, have you got names for them?" The vicar was uninformed. He fidgeted on his platform, apologising for the absence of precise information. He began to call them to prayer for the departed souls but she interrupted him. "Can you tell the likes of us where the Somme is?" she asked, her voice edged with righteous radicalism.

Tea and biscuits were provided to becalm them, to compensate them, but most people left the church hall in a daze, hurrying to the shops in search of a late edition of the local newspaper. My mother would not see the food wasted and stayed behind. Hunger had been her lot for as long as she could remember, each hard-earned potato and piece of meat devoured to the last scrap. Norman came up to her and made timid conversation. The mug in his hand trembled as he sipped the tea without relish.

"How come you're not at war?" my mother asked him, alarmed at his malnourished frame. He was short, with greasy dark hair and shifty eyes. She found him unattractive but was intrigued by his immaturity.

"They need us digging coal, else I'd be off. Dunno for sure, do you?"

"Who are your parents? I've not seen you this way before?"

"Harris is my dad's name, Bill. Mum's Agnes, she's down with arthritis. We only moved to Accrington last month. We got evicted from York, Dad couldn't pay the rent. Accrington's dirt cheap, and he got a job in the colliery office sorting out the wages."

"Any more kin?"

"One brother, Stan, but he left home as soon as he grew long enough legs, going to sea, he said. We've not heard from him since. And what about you?"

"There's only me, I'm eighteen next Thursday. You can take me out if you want."

He slurped at the cup to disguise his happiness.

They spent a cold October afternoon wandering through the marketplace, inspecting the goods on offer, but with no purpose and no means of buying anything. Norman was short on conversation. He stopped at a butcher's window, gazed in and muttered something meaningless about the meat chops on display. "Pretty they are," he said. She looked at the chops, freshly cut, still leaking blood, and grimaced. "Let's go to the football park, it's lonely there at this time," she said, walking off, not bothering to wait for him. He had come empty-handed. She wanted to be taken to the tea-shop for a treat. Instead he took her on a tiresome journey from shop window to shop window.

They sat on the wooden pavilion bench, she pulling the top of her overcoat tightly across her neck, he clapping and rubbing his hands to ward off the chill. Darkness came thickly. She moved to the far end of the bench to avoid the smell of his cheap after-shave.

"What's the matter?" he asked weakly.

"Nothing, I just want to be by myself and watch the stars coming out." They sat apart waiting for the clouds to shift but no star was visible. "Norman, do you think there's anything to anything?"

"How do you mean?"

"I don't know myself, but last year when I was seventeen I came here by myself. The sky sparkled then, made me feel rich, but the more I stared the more I started to doubt. I felt rich to begin with, as if I could wrap the sky around my body with all its jewellery, but the longer I stayed the more my belly grumbled. I spoke to the moon and all her bright-eyed children, so many thousands and thousands of stars, like the greatest glittering royal family in the whole universe, making ours look cheap as coal. I spoke out, I asked them, will there be more to my life than potato and a little meat? Norman, do you ever ask yourself what more there is?"

Norman cleared his throat, unsure of her intent. "To tell the truth, I can't remember the last time I looked up. When you're underground you're mostly crouching, the roof's low, there's dust everywhere, even if you looked up there's bugger all to see so I suppose I've got into the habit of crouching with my eyes lowered…" He paused to think at what he had uttered, surprised at his awakening to self-knowledge. Before her question he had never been motivated to examine his way of looking at the world, much less at himself.

"You're a clever one, Maureen, educated like. I don't rightly know nothing."

There was such a sadness in his voice that she took pity on him, moving to sit beside him. She took his hand in hers, to give warmth to it. His mouth moved towards her but she turned away, his clumsy lips barely grazing the side of her face. He coughed again, out of panic.

"Oh, I'm starving, Norman, why didn't you buy me a cake for my birthday?" Norman started to make apologies for his insufficiency but she brushed them aside. "Serves you right if they conscript you! When you set off, stuff your pockets with dried meats, dried fruits, anything that will swell in your belly, for they will despatch you to some lean field in France. Then a German bayonet will open you up, the rats will come in to eat what's left inside you. They'll roost and breed in their Norman-belly hotel but not pay you any rent but rat dung. But that's all you're worth anyway, that's what they pay you at pit, isn't it?"

Norman braced himself for another assault but her anger was spent. Her gloom was almost palpable. "I did get you a birthday present," he said, to raise her spirits. He fumbled in his coat pocket and retrieved a crumpled piece of paper. She unfolded it slowly, in a show of anticipation to please him, but a tooth was revealed, and she could barely conceal her horror. He picked it up and held it high to catch whatever light there was.

"It's got gold in the cavity. It's me grannie's. She got the rot dug out and replaced with gold, specially for her wedding to grandad. When she died grandad had it taken out from her mouth before they buried her. It's our heirloom. My father inherited it, and now it's yours. Go on, keep it."

He pressed the tooth into her hand. She stared at it as she would stare at the moon and stars, the same incomprehension mingled with sadness. "Norman, is this your way of asking me to marry you? Are you proposing to me?"

The idea hadn't entered his mind but he found himself saying yes. She leaned towards him and kissed him on the lips, withdrawing before he could respond. She looked up to the blankness of the sky. "You'd think a star, even a dull or half-blind one, would appear to witness our romance, but not a thing!"

"Tomorrow night they'll be out. We can always come back tomorrow night," he said.

They returned to the football park the next evening and made love, defying the emptiness of the sky. She was in a sparkling mood, and though he could not always follow her meaning he was content to be still, to simply listen to her. He was overwhelmed by her superior understanding of things. As she talked he picked the residue of sex from her back and shoulders, pieces of grit which had fastened to her when he had pressed her to the pavilion bench.

"I'll marry you as soon as I'm pregnant. Then they'll not send you to war."

"Why not?"

"Because they made a law about it, I read it in the papers. I suppose after the war there'll be a great need for new babies who will grow up to do all their dirty work and fight their new wars."

"Who are they?" he asked, no longer caring to conceal his stupidity.

"They're the ones who teach us what to believe in. You rarely see them. They are invisible to the likes of us because they're in their mansions, they're in parliament or in other places we can't get to, places without windows, or with windows so high we can't peep in. But we'll beat them in the end, won't we?"

"We will," he agreed.

"And do you know why?"

"I don't, but you said, so we're bound to win."

She laughed, drew him to her and kissed him deliciously. "Your brawn and my brain will do the trick. I'll direct the battle and you'll charge and scatter them. You'll be my knight of the Round Table, like olden days."

"I'm not sure you should trust my strength," he said, feeling his muscles, acknowledging his puny talent.

"You think I'm clever, but I'm not. You only have to read a little to discover the world. The newspapers tell of revolution in Russia. And down south women are fighting for the vote, chaining themselves to railings, jumping in front of men's horses. Accrington's nothing today, a piece of grime, but it wasn't always so you know."

"Now you're going too far! What else could it have been?"

"No, honest, I read it in a book. A silly book for sure but it said that long before the pits and the chimneys there was forest. People lived in a little clearing, beside a stream. There were deer and trout. Women wove mats from reeds, made clay pots, clothes from the fur of animals, wine from wild berries. I read in the book about a time of plenty, and though there were kings and knights and castles, no-one interfered with their daily lives. In fact the knights would visit the village and sit peacefully with folk, telling them wonderful stories of going abroad to conquer monsters and Moors, of having to cross dangerous swirling rivers with only their lovers' handkerchiefs to keep them company, to keep their courage afloat. That's why they held tournaments, training to tilt with lance and sword. The village women would give them herbs before they left, instructing them on the healing properties of tansy or rosemary, how to boil and mix them into a paste to rub on aches and wounds. In olden days Accrington was like the sound of gilded harps, not what blares out from Salvation Army brass, and the knight-class of people lived in peace with simpler folk. But I'm prattling on about a silly book, are you bored yet?"

"Bored? I could stay here forever to hear you out. You're like one of those knights full of strange stories. Honest, I don't mind that I don't have my own mind, you know, don't bother if I'm tongue-tied, you just talk."

"But don't you wish you could be one of those knights and me one of those ladies? Or, if that's too much, we could have been sturdy like our forebears in the forest, not hunched underground or stiff with arthritis as folk are now."

"All that's gone now, don't we just have to manage with what's left…?" he asked with uncertainty.

"Nothing's gone if it remains in the mind, and you're mindful of it," she said, her fierceness of tone stilling Norman. "Promise me you won't ever give up on what's in my mind, and become nobody, and make me become nobody."

"I won't give up on you, if that's what you want, but you must tell me what it is that I mustn't give up, otherwise I'll give up out of ignorance."

She laughed at his effort at prolonged speech. "You're a little monkey, Norman, that's what you are. Look at you picking grit from my skin like how a monkey picks lice from its mother's fur!" He was wounded by her disdain and yet seduced by it. He resolved to marry her, and with the authority that came with being husband of the household, he would sink her, pull her down to his level of being. Her knights voyaged overseas to face adversity, he would stay at home in ordinary Accrington and conquer her. He would make her surrender to his will, as she did earlier in their love-making, clutching at his body as to a log in a dangerous swirling river, her passion rising to the surface, desperate to remain alive. If he wanted he could have withdrawn and let her go, but he remained inside her, prolonging her desire for life.

"I'll never give up on you, I'll support whatever it is you want," he lied.

She knew he was lying but didn't care. The dreams would remain in her mind, intimations of knightly romances in magical lands and of common folk at home settled and peaceful in their forest dwelling; dreams that came to her in bed, keeping her awake so that she moved through the daytime hours with a sense of unreality, her dazed state causing people to gossip behind her back. "She's an odd 'un that Maureen, like she's seen a ghost." "She's becoming a woman, she needs marrying like a cow needs milking or she'll go mad." "What man will want a strange thing like that in his bed? She'll have to settle for a pauper like her father."

"Last night I put your grandmother's tooth under my pillow and waited for a fairy to appear, but none did. I wanted the fairy to tell me to dream that I had planted the tooth in our garden and a vine grew overnight, laden with berries. If you sucked away the flesh a golden seed was left behind. I sold all the seeds to a passing merchant and made so much money that I called the whole of Accrington to a banquet. Huge legs of cured ham, roasted lamb, gallons of spirits and all the foods we can't get because of who we are, and the war and all. News quickly spread, hordes of folk believing in a miracle made a pilgrimage to Accrington from all parts of Lancashire and Yorkshire, and even from down south. I gave to them all, I didn't want anything for myself, and no praise either, for I closed my ears when they called me wondrous. If you don't believe me ask the moon and stars, they saw it all, they see all my dreaming. But the fairy didn't come, and no miracle happened…" She stared at him, accusing him for the emptiness of the sky, knowing that when she married him a black cloth would be wrapped around her face, though it still would not cloud her inner sight and she would defy the emptiness of him, the barren tooth, the absence of the fairy.

"Never mind," he said, reading her thoughts with unusual clarity. "We'll keep the tooth for a rainy day." No longer had he spoken than a shower descended, unusually heavy for an October evening. They hurried home, both glad that the noise and fullness of the rain made conversation impossible.

*

The tooth was the last thing Norman pawned. He smashed it, retrieved the lump of gold, and took it to the shop. He felt guilty raising hammer to tooth, as if he was murdering his grandmother, but the mood soon passed as he spied the crystal ball nestling in a cobwebbed corner of the pawnshop. Murder? Why should he feel more guilty than the next man? Maureen was right – war was mass-murder, millions had their skins soaked in other people's blood. And Maureen was right again when she asked whether there was more to life than lumpy potatoes and a scrap of meat. There was not. That was all there was, and he, Norman, would put a knife to any man's throat to ensure he got his portion of whatever life slopped in his direction. For a moment the thought of violence fired him up, he imagined himself behind a machine-gun in the fields of the Somme, massacring the enemy, and afterwards a parade, a ceremony, and the white-gloved hand of authority pinning a hero's medal to his chest to the polite applause of a select audience. The dream flickered and died, he found himself the disappointment he always was to Maureen: a short unsightly unemployed man with no prospect of self-improvement. He caught sight of his reflection in the crystal ball and stared at its unwholesomeness. He fumbled to steady the ball in his hand, suppressing his self-disgust. Maureen would save him. She had imagination. He could dream now and again about chivalry but he awoke too quickly. Life put a knife to his throat and jolted him back, with brutal swiftness, to his paltry self. Maureen had imagination though, life couldn't bully her into submission to her ordinary self. Maureen was not herself. The neighbours gossiped that she was mad, and they were right, for Maureen believed in knights, villages of plenty, and a past that was paradise. Happily he exchanged the untoothed gold for the crystal ball, for it was certain that Maureen would gaze into them and see gorgeous shapes, pictures in the freshest colours which could banish even the drabness of Accrington. Maureen would mine the layers of dirt and failure that had overlaid Accrington for centuries and discover the treasury of ancient courts.

*

"Accrington. It means place of acorns," she told him, looking out of the dingy pub to the Salvation Army band. She beamed when she repeated the word acorns. Their wedding surroundings were hardly romantic, but the word aroused her by its evocation of idyll. She was now with husband, and two months pregnant. The beer was flat, the wedding company stank of tobacco smoke, the band was brassily funereal, but there was idyll on her tongue. The word acorns tasted of apricot and honeydew and sloe and the wetness of green fields. "I'm in bud," she whispered in Norman's ear, feeling for the small lump in her belly, and Norman looked shyly at her, lacking the courage to acknowledge his virility. "We tilted, your lance broke inside me and now you are my vanquished warrior," she said, not minding when he looked stupidly at her. There would be time enough to bring him to brightness of mind. For now she would send him underground to work extra shifts to heap up money sufficient for the promise she made to the unborn child, of a house set in a rich garden, a house with panels and beams and memories of acorns.

The promise, though it was never fulfilled, lived within her like a brood of surly children. Soon after I was born she moved away from Norman's bed, the two of us sleeping in a tiny back room. She never shared her nakedness with him again. She gave her life over to nurturing the promise, guarding it from the grime she saw when she gazed into the crystal ball. Norman wanted stories that would excite the audience, make them empty their pockets more readily, but all she told were tales of woe. Some came to a session of scrying hoping for good news from their dead ones, perhaps a tip for the Derby race or the winning numbers of the local lottery; others came wanting to know where Jack had buried the money from the Post Office robbery (if there was any left), or what John had done with his dad's medals from the Boer War since they were worth a packet now. They looked to their dead ones to verify ownership of a box of carpenter's tools, a bicycle, pots of paint, for there were constant quarrels within families over the contents of the sheds of the bereaved. Maureen's crystal ball gave off an invisible spiteful vapour which she breathed in with relish. She filled her lungs, blew into their faces stories of their iniquities. From their hunched and eager position, eyeing the ball curiously, they started back, nearly toppling from their chairs.

The usual arguments raged after each session, Norman apoplectic at the loss of income because of Maureen's indiscretions in revealing those of others. Maureen shrugged off his protests and took to her solitary bed. She didn't care that her client base was dwindling. Norman bullied her to resume her work, using me – then a four year old – as bait and blackmail. I was shoeless, clothed in rags. Soon I would have to attend school, he pleaded, I would need a school uniform, slate and sufficient food to nourish my growing brain. Maureen relented, new clients came, our parlour was once again populated with the destitute and the superstitious. Norman changed his position, standing behind Maureen, looming over her so that she could sense the threat of his presence. It also offered him a better view of the young widows' cleavages as they leaned forward to catch Maureen's whispers, her voice lowered in the effort to restrain truth-telling of her clients' misdeeds. To begin with she lied boldly and with clear enunciation, like a general condemning lesser men to death in futile battles by the prospect of victory. When she tired of lies she was tempted to blast them with the cannon balls of reality. It was war with her, war, the pall of widowhood hanging densely over Accrington, but she reined in her voice to a wheeze or whisper. In the end she took pity on her clients, surrendering to their needs. She told of husbands with the name of their wives on their dying lips; brave honourable men, faithful to their wives unto death; departed souls who would still keep watch over their families, pulling invisible strings to get this son employed in the quarry, that daughter an apprenticeship in the sewing factory, and in an act of supreme sacrifice (as great as dying for King and Kitchener), finding a new husband for the widow, one with a future, one who wore a white shirt to work.

The money flowed, Norman was a sprightly soul, showing the young clients to the door with a whistle and a wink, making a fuss of refusing money from the pensioners but taking their mite all the same. The years bent double down the pit, the dirt clogging his nostrils, and the occasional explosions which ended life abruptly, convinced him that nothing mattered but his own survival. There was nothing to believe in, there was no God, there was only thirst in the sky and rumbling in his belly. He took the widow's mite without the least pang of conscience. Soon, Maureen made so much money that he splashed out by purchasing a bath, a huge enamel thing, the size of two coffins in width, and with brass taps. He built a brick extension to our kitchen to house it, a space directly below his bedroom. He let people in our street use it, charging sixpence for men and up to three children, and in a gesture of altruism and belated contribution to the war effort (which gained him praise and gratitude, so that he became something of a celebrity in our neighbourhood), nothing for widows. One day I wandered into his bedroom to find him crouching on the floor, his face touching it, like a Muslim at prayer. One hand steadied him, the other was sheathed in his trouser pocket. He bolted upright and shooed me away. When he left the house I entered his room and I discovered the hole he had made in a floorboard to peep at the women bathing.

Mum's spirits sustained us for several years after the war, so that throughout the twenties we lived comfortably. Dad was able to advertise her services in the *Accrington Observer*, the first time she appeared in the newspapers. He invested in a motor scooter to travel outside our immediate vicinity to broadcast Mum's business. He dropped leaflets through doors, granting discounts for multiple visits and, as an added inducement, offering to deliver and return widows on the vehicle. He struck upon an ingenious plan to supplement his income by holding Bible study sessions once a month, in the days when Mum was indisposed and claimed that male spirits (those whom war had transformed into a bloody pulp) would not appear during her menstrual cycle. Of course the Bible study sessions would be free, but a little money could be made from the provision of tea and cakes. Dad was barely literate, so he would organise the donation tin for the refreshments whilst Mum led the readings and exegesis. Those who wanted could stay for a bath afterwards, to complete their cleansing of body and soul, and he could charge a little more for the use of towel and soap. The plan involving clairvoyance and cleansing – "a comprehensive service for the bereaved", as it appeared in the newspaper advertisement – worked, the shillings multiplied faster than Jacob's sheep, and I would peep through the keyhole to see my father in his strange posture on the bedroom floor, a toad-like Moor aroused by vision, preparing to leap into pagan space. I was innocent then of darkness of motive, thinking nothing bizarre about his behaviour – after all I was living in a house of visiting oddballs; widows of all ages and sizes, flat-footed or high-heeled, perfumed or musty to the nose, sobbing or giggling or farting or fainting at my mother's revelations.

The plan worked until tragedy struck during an examination of a passage from Leviticus. Mum was going on about how the Lord had instructed the Jews to prepare a lamb offering (how to cut the throat with the right hand, open up the belly with the left hand, poke out the eye with the third finger of the right hand, scoop out the entrails and throw them into the fire with the left hand, but with the thumb nestled in the palm, keeping its innocence for another most sacred task, that of feeling in the lamb's anus for dung which, when retrieved and scattered on the ground, revealed the Lord's plan for the slaughter of the Hittites) when one of the congregation keeled over and died, though not letting go of the Bible even as she collapsed on the ground. She had not so much as eaten one of the buns Dad had provided as refreshment. Dad roared off on his scooter to call an ambulance, first dropping off one of the women – she was too old for lust, so he felt obliged to charge her a halfpenny – on his way to hospital. Those who remained behind awaiting the ambulance kept fanning her, though she was palpably dead, while speculating on the cause of her going. She had not eaten anything, so it was not a case of choking. Nor could it be age – she was only in her thirties. There was no evidence of blood trickling down her leg indicating stillbirth or a botched abortion. By the time the ambulance arrived they had reached a consensus. They blamed it on Leviticus. Disgusting, all that talk of slaughtering meat, carving it up this way and that, draining the blood. True, they ate lamb, but they bought it from the butcher in a few chops which didn't resemble any living creature. The meat could have been growing from trees for all you knew, you couldn't tell it was from a living animal. Leviticus had killed the woman, she must have died from pure nausea at the imagining of blood, a nausea which stopped her heart as brutally as some Jew's knife stopped the heart of that poor lamb. "What are we women but lambs left for slaughter?" one of them cried in sudden illumination, remembering how her man had abandoned her for the adventure of the Somme, abandoned her to life-long scraping and seduction, beggaring her virtue in return for an hour in Dad's enamel bath. "It's the Jews, they're the ones who paid for the war and profited." There was a chorus of assent and one of them spat into the Old Testament.

The years of plenty ended, Mum reverting to honest disclosures. She spoke of the incest she saw, the adultery, the thieving, the back-stabbing, the deceit, the beatings. The catalogue of wickedness, the awareness of human capacity – indeed suitability – for destruction, maimed her spirit. She withdrew to the chastity of her room, refusing to emerge for sessions with the dead. Dust settled on the crystal ball as it settled over her inward eye, and she lost sight of the promise of the great house in its green acres. I was about fourteen when she gave up on us. Dad was at first patient, hoping she would come to her senses and resume business. He bided his time, making ends meet by using his scooter to transport people and parcels around the town, and by encouraging greater use of the bath. I cleaned it dutifully, contributing to the income of the household, but all the time I was nurturing Mum's vision, keeping it shining so that she could acquire it again, when she recovered, as a bright and living promise. I spent my teenage years in the local library, reading productively – the legends of Greece and Rome, the lives of great historical figures, stories of inventions and discoveries that changed the world – as a way of preparing myself for the time when Mum would awaken from her slumber and once more be seized by vision. Dad supported me as best he could, paying one of the neighbours to make my dinner, another to sew my school uniform. He took me to school and back on his scooter. People admired his efforts, pitied him the burden of a sick wife. The house was as busy as ever, women coming not to seek their fortunes but to leave small presents – a vase, a box of candles, a pair of curtains, and more often than not, a handful of coins. One day, a woman called Daisy, one of Mum's previous clients, broke into tears as she emptied her purse into my hand. "I can't go on, he'll finish me off," she sobbed, and I was so alarmed that the coins fell from my hand.

"Pick them up, quick, quick, pick them up, tell him I brought three shillings, all of it. If I'm short, I'm finished." She scrambled to retrieve the coins from the floor.

"Why are you giving us money and why are you crying?" I asked, refusing to take the coins, but she ignored me, placed them on the table and left the house in a panic. When Dad came home I related the incident, but he said nothing, stabbing hungrily at the slices of ham which I had laid out for his supper. He counted the money, and satisfied that it was all there, he pocketed it with a grin.

"You're blackmailing Daisy, are you Dad?" I asked.

He raised his head from his plate and gazed at me curiously. "You've got your mother's gift, that idle bitch passed it on to you didn't she?"

I looked into his eyes, seeing frantic and excited calculation. I remembered Daisy gasping as my mother hurled accusations at her, namely her betrayal of her husband with the pit manager. She had come wanting news of her father who had recently fallen into a pond and drowned, but Mum exposed her infidelity instead. As I looked upon my father, I realised why so many woman were coming to our house bearing gifts. He was threatening to tell the world of what women had got up to when their husbands were away fighting in France or down the pits. Mum had given away their secrets, and Dad had found a new means of making a living.

"You sleep with them as well, that's why Mum flinches when you are near her," I said. I held my breath, expecting him to explode in anger or to protest his innocence, but he merely smiled at me, his face lit in the same rapture of discovery as my mother's when she raised her head from the crystal ball.

"You've *definitely* got the gift," he said, the prospect of renewed fortune dawning upon him.

That night I didn't sleep with my mother. I made a bed in the parlour, the space of her performances, the closeness to the crystal ball making me feel protective of her. I would watch over them until she awoke to become my mother again, resisting the mean spirit of my father.

*

I was about fourteen when Mum withdrew into herself and Dad first thrust the crystal ball into my hand, insisting that I make contact with the spirits. I looked into it but saw only the face of my mother, which was like my own. High forehead, thin lips, dimpled chin, slender nose, hazel-coloured eyes, naturally curly auburn hair, shoulder length, parted in the middle. "What a pretty child, just like your mother," the clients used to tell me when I let them into the house.

"What do you see?" my father growled, but I would not tell him that I was looking at a woman whose high forehead suggested an intelligence beyond his, and whose frail and beautiful presence was in such contrast to his uncouthness.

"Look properly," he urged. "You've inherited your Mum's gift." He relented when my eyes misted in sorrow. He relieved me of the ball, but I was crying not because of any threat from him but because of the despoliation of my mother's face, its mask of madness and the evidence of self-neglect in her dirt-encrusted cheeks. For all her fresh maidenly appearance in the crystal ball she was in reality an unclean and rapidly ageing thing. She would stay locked in her room for days, and I became like her gaoler, putting a tray of food outside, emptying her pot of urine in the morning. She emerged only when Dad was out of the house and I was in school. I would come home to find water on the kitchen floor. She had washed herself in the kitchen sink, refusing the enamel bath. One evening, when blood was sticky on my thighs for the first time, I took a bath. I heard the creaking of floorboards and looked up to imagine Dad prostrate at his peep-hole. Soon, I knew, I too would become one of his widows.

He never troubled me for months, not until I was fifteen or so. Once more the crystal ball was shoved in my direction, and his face quivered impatiently as he awaited word from me. "Look for Daisy, tell me what she's up to," he urged, his mouth almost watering with anticipation. There was a ravenous look in his eyes, like a dog starved of affection. Daisy had stopped coming to the house for some time. In fact the many women who came to leave tribute had eventually lessened to a trickle and then to an occasional presence.

"They've given up on you, you don't get much from them any more," I told him, not even bothering to peer into the magic glass. For a moment he looked forlorn, then his eyes quickened with approval, for he was pleased by my gift of mysterious sight.

"Go on, go on," he begged.

"Soon you'll get nothing, your income will dry up." I suspected that Daisy and the others had, with the passage of years, grown apathetic to Dad's threats to expose them. Or else they just didn't have the money to pay – the time of shortage and unemployment was upon Accrington once more – and preferred shame to starvation. Some moved out of the area, out of Dad's reach. Some who got pregnant by him and bore his children argued that he had got enough out of them, especially since their unsuspecting husbands were footing the bills for the new mouths. The odd one, already abandoned by her man for other reasons, stayed faithful to him, giving her pound of flesh because the sex was pleasurable and even if it was not, the routine of a Thursday night tussle in the back-garden shed remained a stubborn ruttish compulsion.

"Daisy's sick, you've given her a sickness," I lied, hoping to provoke his compassion and stop his harassment of her. He dared not protest, for I was in possession of the crystal ball. I could have hurled it at him, crushing his head, but I knew my utterance would do more damage to his mind.

"You are to leave them alone, cease your threats or else you'll be done in. Some of their men are growing suspicious, they'll surprise you, prise you open, one of them will cripple you with a crowbar one dark night."

He breathed heavily, in grief and frustration. "Can't you see any good? Is it all gloom and doom? Why do you have to be like your mother and ruin me with nasty stories?"

I may have saved Daisy and the others from further abuse, but it proved to be an act of sacrifice, for Dad's behaviour towards me changed. He used to be kind and fatherly, ensuring I had enough to eat, cleaning the house so that when I returned from school I had a pleasant environment in which to do my homework. He even sawed and hammered together planks of wood to make me a comfortable bed in the parlour, so I didn't have to endure the squalor of Mum's room. Every now and again he would present me with a pleasing trinket from the pawnshop, a necklace or a purse to keep me cheerful, seeing that I had an apathetic and neglectful mother. Now, my exposure of his cruelty to Daisy and other women made him tyrannical towards me. He began to isolate me from all contact with life outside his control. Apart from going to school or to the library I was not to leave the house, to protect me from the danger of meeting boys of my age, or girls who would set a bad example by their vulgar ways. I was to be kept in a virginal and secluded state, so that my powers of prophecy could develop without interference of the outside world. He squatted over me with rank thighs, waiting for me to chip through my shell and chirp out greetings to folk hungering for transfiguration, folk who didn't want to hear what they were but what they ought to have been. And somehow, by the mystery of utterance, I was to deceive them into believing that they knew not what they did, or did not whereof they knew. Mum had refused him, vicious in her unveiling of their sins, but I was being prepared for acts of masking. I was to wear the mask of innocence, to see better the nature of their unlived experiences; lives that could have been fortunate before they became wasted and deprived. But the folly of his project was obvious even to one of my age: how could Accrington, with its pits, factories, open sewers and ingrained habits of scavenging, hold out the prospect of fortune to anyone? Still, I surrendered to his will, for it saved me from the shame of acknowledging I had no friends, no girls who would invite me to their houses after school or to the ice-cream parlour on a Saturday afternoon. Boys never made suggestions to me, never offered me cigarettes and bottles of beer, never took me to the woods afterwards. It was because I was my mother's child, a person acquainted with ghosts. They were afraid of the invocations of the dead. I must have smelt to them of wreaths and pine-coffins and cheap perfume sprinkled on the bodies of the departed; or worse, of corpses breaking through the earth, resurrected in maggoty form.

Home was refuge and salvation from such scorn. At an early age I knew I would never marry but was destined for an inward life; and destined to tend to my parents in their peculiar calling.

The teachers often praised me for my brightness, and even wanted me to stay back after school for special lessons, but I preferred the security of my home. I set about cleaning with maniacal zeal, doing religious battle with grime and coal-dust. Looking after Mum meant wiping her down with wet cloths, turning her over to prevent bedsores, tipping food into her mouth and reading to her passages from books I had borrowed from the library. Books were my abiding companions for there was little response from Mum. She was too withdrawn into her nightmares to acknowledge me. The dead had visited their maladies unto her. The odd flicker of recognition from her made me renew my efforts to awaken her to ambition.

Dad had given up on whatever little ambition he ever possessed. I was his only portal to the future. He pawned whatever had value in the house, including the enamel bath, then sold his scooter, making ends meet and biding his time until I was ripe for the visitation of spirits.

*

Men came. His Accrington pals. Why did he bring them? Was it to dilute the guilt of his offence by sharing it with others? Like men going over the trench en masse to be mown down together? It was partly for the money, for his pockets bulged with notes and coins from my nightly endeavours. The real reason was to appease Harold, a retired banker who ran the local office conscripting able-bodied men for the war. Harold's authority lay in his history of dealing with money but also in his eye-patch which reminded people that he was once a high-ranking officer who was wounded but survived the Somme and received a shiny medal for his lost eye. Harold, with the stroke of a pen, could consign men to the new battlefields, so Dad, to dodge the war, offered me instead to his service.

The men – all elderly – turned up in groups of three or four. I was clumsy to begin with but grew more and more accomplished with experience, learning how to identify and satisfy their individual and collective fantasies, how to tease or appease, how to protest or acquiesce. Harold would preside over the gambolling of the paedophiles, to ensure the quality of my performance but also to protect me against their excess, for many times he would holler to this one or that to desist from whatever act of biting or stretching made me call out in pain. Harold himself never breached me but looked on kindly, his good eye twinkling. Afterwards, he counted out the money without looking, for money was second-nature to him. His eye was fixed on me, his face a rosy smile, as his fingers tallied what was due to Dad. When the pals departed, Dad would come and lie beside me, seeking the shelter of my swollen breasts, and I would listen to the drip drip drip of his guilt along my thighs, knowing that in the morning he would chastise me with blows to the head. My whole body remained aroused for hours after the pals left. My nipples were stiff with longing, for the pals were too old to satisfy me fully, but Dad would not enter me, so I lay awake anticipating the stars that would glow in my mind when daylight came; an unnatural shining, for stars, like men, were creatures of the night.

From the age of fifteen and into my twenties I was wife to Dad's select band. I grew to be subtle, animate, consummately skilled under Harold's stewardship. He usurped whatever natural authority Dad held over me. Sometimes Dad would slip away when the pals arrived, returning very late and retreating to his bed. He would spend all day on his own, waiting for darkness to make his escape. He no longer entered me. The beatings stopped. Talk between us dwindled into monosyllables. I sensed his need to keep distant from me, but to punish him I would often insist he remained in the parlour, out of fatherly duty, to keep watch over the pals in case Harold gave them too much allowance. To punish him, but also to restore his pride by acknowledging that he, not Harold, was the final arbiter.

During those years my mother declined slowly, became so wasted that she could barely lift her head from her pillow. The stench of her decay spread like a miasma throughout the house, no amount of bleach or burnt sandalwood could banish it. I fed her when I could, but stopped reading the Bible to her: there was too much housekeeping to do, especially now that Dad had re-stocked the house with furniture and retrieved the enamel bath from the pawn-shop. It had been too big for the premises, the proprietor placed it in his garden, covered over with tarpaulin, which offered scant protection from nature. It had fallen on its side. Rain trickled in, making dirty veins in the sides. Beetles and slugs copulated, leaving stains and dropping dung which corroded its surface. It was hell to restore it to its original state, but I persisted in scrubbing and polishing, wanting it to be so pristine that I could see my mother's face in it.

*

Two years into the Second World War, and the air raid sirens called to Mum. She got out of bed early one morning, shook me tenderly. I opened my eyes in panic, expecting Dad's violence. "Ssh, ssh, ssh," she said drawing me to her, and I nestled my head to her breast. In a flash I reverted back to the time of promise, when we both hoped for another life in another place. She led me to the enamel bath, washed me, took me upstairs, dressed me in white cotton, oblivious of the passage of the years. "Jesus wants me for a sunbeam," she sang as she put on her green dress patterned with red flowers, examining herself approvingly in the mirror. "Sweet Molly, let's go gather berries and toadstools, it's bright and fresh outside," she said taking my hand and leading me out of the house to a patch of woodland at the edge of town.

I remember the scent of wet grass and greenery. The mist lifted to show an earth speckled with flowers and acorns; the flowers asleep, stilled in infancy and unbearably fragile; the acorns lying quietly where they had fallen on the ground, awaiting natural growth. My mother stooped to gather mushrooms, twirling each before my face as if to delight me by its odd stalk, rim, crevices, before placing it in her basket. I remember her walking through the woods in her green dress – she resembled a plant which could move magically from spot to spot. I remember a green plant bearing red flowers gliding along the earth, entranced by its own wizardry, its freedom to move from this joyous space to that, no longer manacled by its roots. The plant stopped, bowed to the earth, sent out shoots to explore the undergrowth, then the flash of explosion, as if my father had crept up behind me and cuffed my head, causing light to dazzle me, to blind me to remembrance of his blighting of me. Fingers of light plucked out my eyes, scraped clean the insides of my sockets. I stumbled through the brightness calling out to my mother in a fledgling voice, craving the dark protective down of her body.

At the funeral I wept in hatred of her. The newspapers said she failed to foretell her death, but she knew all along about the doings of the pals, she gave me over to Dad's ambition as a way of abandoning her own. I was deceived that morning she took me to the woodland. I had wanted to believe that she had regained her vision and ambition, and I surrendered to her motherhood of me, letting her wash me, dress me, sing to me. Instead she was determined to humiliate me, lower me to her level of sickness and doubt. She had succeeded for my body was now injured at the hip.

On the day of the funeral Dad's appetite for me returned. He made me shave my pubic hair so that I would remain child-like in spite of my woman's breasts. He organised a wake, with provisions as meagre as those of his wedding day. It was 1941, food was scarce, his pals had to do with the butcher's leftovers. There was plenty of home-brewed alcohol which I drank as copiously as any of the men. The pain in my hip was numbed, I lay down, spread and stretched for them, wanting to be as delicious as ever. I looked at myself in the mirror Dad had recently fixed on the ceiling, gratified to see how gorgeous my body had grown, nourished by their milk. Afterwards, however, when I stood up to walk I was ungainly, lacking in self-assurance. I imagined the pals sniggering behind my back as I left the parlour to fetch them more beer from the kitchen. "It's a miracle you survived, you're a special one," Dad whispered in my ear, stroking my shaven flesh, trying to arouse it in preparation for more doings with his pals. "You're so special, it's a miracle you survived," he said, but I refused to moisten, steadfast in self-loathing of my hip. Mum had damaged me. I would limp all my life. She had gained cruel revenge over Dad and his men, yielding me up to them as damaged, never to be quite as desirable as before. I brushed away Dad's hand. I glared at the men so fiercely that they withdrew, laughing nervously, looking upon Harold to stifle my disobedience. Dad interrupted whatever decision Harold was intending to make. "There'll be nothing more happening tonight," Dad snarled, turning on them, ordering them from my presence. Harold, sensitive as ever, looked benignly upon Dad and patted him on the back in a show of brotherhood. Dad was pleased by Harold's gesture but deep down he knew his outburst was a false exhibition of authority, for without Harold he would be reduced to beggary and the possibility of dying in some foreign field. My infancy had saved him from the First World War and my womanhood from the Second.

A week later Harold and his pals showed up. Dad led them silently to me, imploring me with his eyes to cooperate. Once more I reduced myself to a piece of meat which the men were contented with, for that was all there was to life. They were elderly, huffing and puffing over me, sinking in their slackened teeth, and afterwards, falling over dazed, desperate to catch their breath. I watched them stalking me, then saddling and mounting me with unsteady gait. I thought of Mum's ancient knights returning from foreign lands without triumph, for there was none to be had, no hoped-for adventures, no epic struggles. They settled for me, a limp thing from Accrington, a dented and undistinguished trophy, an empty grail. Harold gave me a walking stick.

The inevitable happened. One dark night someone crept up behind Dad as I had foretold, weapon in hand. Dad, his head a pulp, managed to struggle to the front door where he collapsed. Only at daybreak was he discovered by men on their way to pit. Three months in hospital, surgery, stitches, bandages, tubes. He drifted into the shadow of death, then summoned up his self, moved it back into the realm of life. When he was eventually discharged from hospital he was permanently disabled, unable to walk, to speak, barely sighted, hands constantly trembling. The same journalist who had reported Mum's death noted Dad's mishap. He would come round to the house to ask questions of me, for he sensed a revelation of shocking deeds in our ordinary Accrington house. I disclosed nothing to him, feigning ignorance as to the reason for the crime committed against my father. He persisted, offering me money, but I refused it. The pals, stunned by the violence done to my father and hearing of the journalist's snooping, stayed away, and for the rest of the war I had peace at night and in the daytime the tranquillity of the silent house. I took care of Dad, undressing and washing him, my familiarity with his body making this task routine, for his nakedness no longer held surprise as on the first night. Sometimes, when I fed him, I would lean over his face so that my breasts dangled like fruit, beyond his reach. He would open his mouth in a futile attempt at speech. I would bring him to the brink of speech, and then desist, letting him collapse back into his silenced self. At last I had power over him, the power of words. Such tantalising was not done solely out of cruelty. A man with his foul appetite for pleasure could so easily succumb to his disability and die. My duty was to lure him to recovery, to seduce him with the belief that his limbs would straighten, his body stop trembling, that he would arise and ejaculate again. My attempts at conjuration failed, he remained immobile and bedridden. Raising the dead was truly beyond me.

I could have summoned the pals to me, for the sake of the rent money, but also to stem my loneliness, for some nights saw me jolt out of sleep, doused in sweat. I found myself craving their company, their lewd adoration and slobber of gratitude. I craved for the afterglow of my body, the sensation of having been pawed and caressed and brought to climax in the presence of my father. Now that he was crippled, unable to officiate, I felt that giving and receiving from the pals would lack the thrill of indecency. I took to pawning to see us through the war, starting with the crystal ball, for removing it from the house would be ridding myself once and for all of the desire for unchristian sex. The last to go was the enamel bath, taken away by the rag-and-bone man on his cart, like a once magnificent steed grown lame, decrepit and useless, abandoned to the knacker's yard.

The war ended and before long the new Labour government set up systems of care for the poor. A nurse was appointed to wait upon my father, freeing me to return to the library and once more lose myself in books. The Leeds Institute, some eighty miles away, opened its doors to mature students showing promise in lieu of formal certificates of achievement. I applied for a place and was astonished not only to be accepted but also to be offered a bursary adequate for lodging and subsistence.

That last morning in Accrington I wandered through the house trying to remember all the dead people Mum had identified as once belonging to it or having a place in it through our purchase of second-hand goods. There was Mark Garnett who drank black tea with two lumps of white sugar in it, and Caroline Collins, lightly bearded, mashing black pudding between toothless gums. There was the blacksmith who made the iron sink, and Joseph Countryman, the lonely suicide whose hands crafted wood with such finesse, hands that eventually succumbed to despair but still tied the hangman's rope with care and method. And many others who had perished so far back that Mum claimed not to be able to retrieve their names. We had inherited their cups and spoons and cooking utensils, things once intimate to them but handed over so casually to the pawn-shop when the time came, the time of need. They in turn would end up in some other household, but would never be *valued*, for their new owners would lack Mum's clairvoyance. I felt a surge of appreciation for Mum, her ability to identify and trace aspects of the past, giving human names and human character to the rusting bent remains of pots and ladles, making a drawer of old household implements suddenly gleam as if it were a treasure chest. A spiritual trove, not of monetary value for the cup in her mind's eye became a goblet or grail, the kitchen knife an ancient huntsman's dagger, and the pieces of metal which formed a latch, a window-catch or a hinge, were fashioned from once chivalric shields, ceremonial swords. I bade goodbye to the ghosts, and then to Dad, bending over him so that he could gurgle at my breasts one last time. I wiped his face and mouth with a piece of white cloth which was once part of Mum's dress, the one she made me wear on the day of her death. It had survived the blast and I had cut it into pieces with which to clean the enamel bath.

The doorbell rang. It was the taxi taking me to the rail station and then to the Leeds Institute. I turned away from Dad in a show of decisiveness, but swiftly and unexpectedly a storm of distress broke over me. I wept and wept, bereft of all sense of self,

41

of dignity and control, and I turned to him again, clinging to him as he did to me during my youthful years, which now seemed to have lasted forever. I was a teenager when it began and in my late twenties when it ended. But his clinging seemed prior to teenage, prior to childhood and infancy, prior to my foetal state, receding even beyond Mum's sense of the ancient into a time beyond time, beyond recollection.

The doorbell rang again, summoning me back to my present self. I removed my arms from his body, wiped my face and assumed a mask of composure. A melancholy sun greeted me when I left the house. I paused for a moment before entering the taxi, wanting to linger in the sun's gloom and to wither away in companionship with my father.

PART 2

October 3rd 1947 – I struggled up three flights of stairs, clutching walking-stick and suitcase. I was so exhausted as I climbed that I feared I would topple over and fall flat on my face. A young man appeared from nowhere, relieved me of my suitcase and led me to my room.

"You should have got one of the porters," he said.

I sank into the nearest chair to catch my breath. "There was only one in the lodge and he was too busy handing out keys so I dared not ask."

The young man (he introduced himself as Terence Scott) was angry on my behalf. "One porter on duty! But it's the first day, there should be half a dozen to help people to their rooms. The rest are probably idling in the canteen."

I was touched by his concern. "It's OK, I'm here now, perhaps it couldn't be helped," I said to becalm him.

"Why didn't you ask for a ground-floor room, didn't you fill out the form before you came, the bit about special requests?" He stared at my feet. "When you're…" He sought a polite word for my condition and made a soothing choice. "When you're incapacitated, they take it into account in allocating rooms–"

"It's not my feet, they're perfect, it's my hip," I said, interrupting his stare and drawing his eyes up my body to my waist. He twitched nervously. "It's the war," I said, and before I could elaborate he spoke out apologetically.

"Quite a few people in college are, em… incapacitated, due to the war."

"Oh?" I was unsure whether to wear a face of surprise or pity. I wanted to please him so I feigned reassurance. "That's good to know, I won't feel odd then."

His skin reddened, he shifted from one foot to the other as if embarrassed by their wholeness. "Damn! I've blown it," I cursed myself. "He'll leave and not come back. You idiot!"

"What about some tea?" I said, pretending not to notice his hesitancy. "I'll go make some in the kitchen. Where is it?"

"No, no, I'll go, you've just arrived, you must be tired."

Once more I found myself basking in his solicitude. "OK then, you go, I'll wait for you," I said, blushing at the hint of coyness in my voice and at the little conspiracy developing between us which could swell and widen into intimacy. I was determined to know him, this fresh-faced teenager with brylcreamed hair parted cleanly on the left but with a hint of unruliness in his slightly extended sideburns. I watched him as he left my room, admiring his purposeful step which suggested the surety of youth, or at least inexperience of war. He returned with two mugs. He pouted his lips and blew at the hot tea and I imagined the scent of his breath, the raw virginity of him. "So you come from far?" he asked and I warmed to his voice, my eyes brightened even as I mentioned the banal word "Accrington".

There were indeed noticeable numbers of disabled people on campus, creaking their way to lessons on cumbersome wheelchairs or hopping across the lawns like bedraggled birds. I was relatively agile, tilting and straightening as I walked. I ignored them, the leftovers of the war, the legless, the broken-backed, the near-blinded, the impotent – not out of malice or contempt but because I wanted to find my own feet, as it were, I wanted to thrive without pity and compensatory kindness from others. I would lean on Terence's body and no other. Lacking perpendicular integrity I would settle for the horizontal, naked and giggling between the sheets.

He lived on the ground floor of my Hall of Residence. Meeting him was as convenient as it was inevitable. We'd settle for tea in my room, in the late afternoon, our first encounter establishing the pattern for future rituals, Terence blowing upon the hot liquid, me stirring in the sugar with exaggerated deliberation, until conversation arose.

"What's her name then?" I asked. Terence looked up from across the table, confused. "Her, the blonde you walk to class with," I said, trying to soften the jealousy in my voice. "She fancies you, I can tell."

"You mean Corinne," he said shyly.

"I can tell by the sway of her hips when you two are going about. And do you notice how she walks lightly, almost on tip-toe?"

"She's nice enough," he said casually as if declaring neutrality in any future hostility between me and Corinne. I could have persisted, probing and foraging through the undergrowth of his desire for Corinne to discover the nature of their relationship, but I relented out of memory of the bomb exploding in my mother's face.

"It's my northern habit, we're not folk for discreet talk, we're direct like," I said to relieve his anxiety. "It's a pretty name, Corinne."

"It is, isn't it."

"Sounds like the countryside wouldn't you say?"

"Apparently she's named after some shepherdess in classical mythology."

"So she's got some class then?" I asked sourly, unable to control my tongue.

Terence sipped his tea so as not to answer. There was a lengthy pause. "She's from Siddon, a village four miles from where I live," he said eventually.

"That's nice for you," I said. "It's good to have two Kent chicks in the deep north, like cuckoos in a stranger's nest. I suppose you must feel a bit out of place."

"That's why we're both here, to get away from all that life, or lack of it."

"Yes, I suppose privilege must be awfully hard to bear, best to slum it up north for a while, a reprieve and a bit of light relief. I was never one for privilege myself, not that it was ever on offer. But there I go again with my tart tongue…"

Terence looked as if he regretted having disclosed his family history to me on the first day, two weeks previously. He had told me that his father was a very senior civil servant, one who did the recruiting and planning rather than the actual fighting. War was so much rustle of paper to him, or the distant drone of bombers flying past their village to drop their load elsewhere, in the industrial cities. His cellar was stocked with cheese, cured meats and beer, there was no need for a ration card. Terence grew up with no sense of shortage. A wealthy father from the landed class; a genteel housewife of a mother whose supervision of decorators and gardeners was her contribution to the war effort. "It's a grand pile, our house, from the eighteenth century," Terence had explained. "Mother thought she was doing her bit for the war just in maintaining the house, keeping it safe for future generations when other places were collapsing under the Luftwaffe. She is a kind of custodian of English heritage, if you see what I mean, guarding it from the barbarians."

I watched him wriggling with embarrassment and felt sorry for him. I took up my stick and poked it at his chest in a gesture of rough northern intimacy. "When are you going to start asking me about me, about time isn't it?"

"What do you want me to ask?" he said, taken aback by my offer.

"Ooh, don't play the innocent with me, young man! Never forget I've got invisible feelers sprouting all over my head, like Medusa's locks. When I look at you I can turn all the chaos of your emotions into stone and rune so I can examine them better. Go on, ask me anything, I'll be your oracle. Don't be shy now."

But he was too shy on this occasion, so I let him be. Our friendship was still young, there would be time enough to bait and bleed him.

He kept returning to my room, twice a week, in spite of my ready tongue. I poked fun at his soft southern background. In between such jibes I told him what he craved, which was vicarious experience of Accrington life. I conjugated Accrington, breaking it down into a series of words to excite his voyeurism. Grit. Acrid. Acid. Axe. Crud. Cruel. Gruel. Rind. Rid. Cringe. "It's a black and white town," I told him, "a place of brutal simplicities," and he was drawn into my fables. "The black is the coal, the white is the light of the smelters and furnaces. But it's not just in coal and metal but in living things. Dad used to fish for eels. He'd chop off the head and string it up over the kitchen sink but it'd still be wriggling and shuddering. They're hard to kill, eels, they don't give up life easily, until Dad boiled water and poured it over the poor thing. The black skin would peel off to reveal white flesh. Mum was fascinated by black and white, and me too, that's why there was all that polishing and scraping and scrubbing in our house. We got our hands dirty trying to restore things to their whiteness."

Terence was as spellbound and appalled as the women who used to visit Mum. He sat across the table as they did, attentive to my evocation of the ghastly and distressing. I never, though, disclosed the doings of Dad and his band of pals. That would wait until I possessed him completely, until he was so enslaved by my siren fables that he could not be emancipated except by my bidding.

*

I peeped at Corinne through my curtains as she walked across the lawn to the lecture theatre, noting the lightness of her tread, the poise of her body. Sometimes she would weave flowers through her blond hair or wear flowing dresses as if to remind herself of her pedigree, shepherdess and sylvan nymph. The classical bitch! I would be siren and Medusa to her Corinne, I'd break her on rocks or turn her into a stony frieze. Terence must have sensed my growing dislike of her and studiously kept her away from me, never bringing her around for tea. He began to take a different route to classes to avoid the two of them passing my window.

"Her's doing the Estate Management course with you, is she?" I asked, cursing the rich under my breath, both studying to profit even more rapaciously from their properties by exerting modern methods of control over their servants. No more Alexander Pope's 'Man of Ross', a poem I was studying just then, which told of ancient bonds of responsibility between lord and peasant, the latter labouring for his master in return for paternal care, a harvest party here, Christmas presents there. Now it was all numbers, a strict accountancy of the servants' wages in relation to levels of efficiency and productivity.

"No, Corinne's actually on the nursing course," Terence said in a revengeful tone. "She's learning how to provide for those crippled by the war." He abandoned the word "incapacitated" in his desire for retaliation. It was the first time I sensed his capacity for spite, an ability to assert his natural superior breeding and status over my kind. "She is no aristocratic angel of mercy," he said, pre-empting any scathing remark from me. "She's not condescending, she's not here to abase herself before the unfortunate in a 'there but for the grace of God and my wealthy parents go I' way. She genuinely cares for people. She could easily have gone to Cambridge to study medicine but she chose a more humble career in a lesser institution like the Leeds Institute. Actually she comes from a family of priests." This declaration of her virtuousness was meant to placate me but I resented her even more. Not only was she beautiful but her breasts leaked the milk of human kindness.

"Do you sleep with her?" I blurted out.

Terence was flustered by the directness of the question although he'd got accustomed to my bluntness. "No I don't," he answered quietly, almost in a whisper. "She's young, more so than you." Again the hint of his potential for unkindness which I regretted and relished at the same time. "You don't like her, do you?" he asked after a while, stating the obvious.

"Nowt to do with it, liking. We're a hard lot, us from Accrington. We've grown up on suet and kidney soup and leftovers from the butcher's. We kick a ball as vicious as we kick in heads, brawling on a Saturday night. Do you know that a small town like ours raised a whole battalion during the First War, thinking to wallop the Huns? The Accrington Pals they were called, and they kicked a ball before them when they poured over the trenches and headed for the Huns, as if war was a bruising derby against Berlin United. The Berliners wiped them out, the final score was Accrington lost by six hundred odd goals, ghouls, souls. Ninety percent of the Pals who took to the field ended up stretchered off. The coach, the manager and the chairman of the club, those buggers were OK, because they stayed on the sidelines in their safe VIP boxes."

"I've never heard about the Accrington Pals," Terence said, and was surprised when I broke into a dark laughter.

"Oh, there's lots more to tell but stay a goof for a while, you're young but your time of knowing will come." And to increase his confusion I added, "When I'm ready for you."

There was not much to Terence. A callow character but harmless. He would always have money in his pockets when he walked out of his home into the street and into his motorcar. The wife would have made him his breakfast, straightened his tie and picked a piece of fluff from his jacket before he left for the office.

A reasonably happy couple, living reasonable lives, with a group of like-minded friends from which to select godfathers and godmothers for their children. Contentment would be their lot, and in church they would give sincere if shallow thanks for their sheltered being, for not being brought to undue suffering. How to unjoin their hands, how to break their circle of mediocrity, became my obsession. I watched Corinne from near and from afar, the wind lifting her hair in a coruscation of light. She was so fair, so pristine. Accrington blondes never caused me jealousy. Somehow the glow of their hair, so mysterious, so beguiling, was negated by low foreheads, jaws too narrow or square, or ill-shaped in some inexplicable way. Even if they were well-proportioned, their beauty was negated the moment they opened their mouths, the crudity or inarticulacy of speech worsened by the drawl of our Accrington accent. Corinne was different. Whatever sunlight there was in the cloud-sodden sky illuminated her hair, her slender face, her unblemished skin, the paleness of which made her seem unearthly. I would see her coming towards me outside the lecture theatre and be dazzled by the perfection of her appearance, the classically chiselled face with its drapery of light, and her skin's milky-white purity. I imagined some ragged ruddy lice-ridden heavy-waisted cock-eyed bone-headed bare-footed peasant, bearing about her the smell of cow-dung and potato blight, suddenly meeting the Virgin Mary, squinting intensely at the apparition, her foul breath stopped in fright and wonder. When Corinne approached she was that apparition of divinity, bathed in light, and me, the figure of mud. Corinne didn't recognise me as she passed by, Terence not having introduced us, but I imagined that her speech would have been as gentle and cadenced as his, if she had stopped to greet me.

A normal young man would be expected to shun my company, the poison of my spittle as I complained about social injustice, but Terence braved my ill-temper. I called him gormless, I called him a ninny and a muggins, but more often than not they were terms of endearment, for I was as entranced by his innocence as I was bent on the spoiling of it. I fed his curiosity about northern life with an aggregation of clichés, telling him about our famous football club; the smell of carbolic in our houses; women wearing wooden clogs which after a shift in the looms sounded over the cobbled streets like a downpouring of hailstones; factory-hooters; men called "knockers-up" armed with long poles which they tapped on windows to wake up mill workers for the dawn shift. I named our household belongings, the oil-lamps, jugs and tin instruments. Our local linguistic idiosyncrasies amused him, our "hey-up" and "give-over" (BBC Radio had no northern voices so he grew up unaware of our mangling and strangling of the language). I looked forward to his visits for our conversations were full of laughter and the delight of an accidental intimacy between people destined to be strangers to each other because of social rules. On Tuesdays and Thursdays I would bathe in preparation for his coming, comb my hair, clean my room, polish the mugs, put fresh sheets on the bed with the nervous anticipation of a novice, a schoolgirl in a crush, ignoring the indictment of my walking stick and the wrinkles around my eyes and mouth threatening to betray my unnatural ageing. Twenty-nine going into thirty but men had laid hands upon me, spoiling not healing.

One afternoon he didn't turn up, leaving me desperate and lonely for the rest of the day and all the next. I went to bed with a tearfulness of a rejected schoolgirl, and could not rouse myself in the morning to attend lectures on Keats and Wordsworth. Theirs was bookish, a suave and rhymed Romance, mine rattled my heart more hideously than clogs over cobblestone at the end of the factory shift.

"Corinne's been ill in bed for a few days," he said by way of an apology when he eventually showed up. "Nothing dreadful but I've been worried all the same."

"There's nothing serious about a rash, it comes with the fever which will pass soon."

"How did you know?" he asked, creasing his brow in surprise.

"Know what?"

"What was wrong with her? It could have been 'flu or swollen glands or anything but you said a rash and fever!"

"Oh, only a guess," I said nonchalantly, disguising the emotion in my voice. "It's only the northern air, the dust creeps into your pores and brings on a fever." To lighten his disbelief I added, "Most of my teenage was spent in bed scratching and tossing. When I was that age I was always in a muck sweat." The lie (a partial one, for Dad's pals did often leave me soaked, their emanations making my skin break out in rashes) satisfied him, but I had to hide my excitement over Corinne's condition by babbling on about Mrs Gaskell's novels ("full of people coughing their lungs up because of injustice and coal dust") which I had been studying that week. "Good thing you didn't come round, I had heaps of reading to catch up on." The truth was that I could barely concentrate on Mrs Gaskell, starting at each footstep in the corridor, thinking it his. When he failed to appear I fretted to begin with, then in slow rage began to curse Corinne. I wished sickness upon her, running through my mind a catalogue of ailments before settling for a rash. It would start in the region of her belly and slowly creep up her chest. I would not make it painful for there was no malignancy in me. Her rash would be irritable, but more importantly unsightly, and the longer Terence stayed away from my presence, the more it would spread to her neck and eventually her face, causing such horror when she looked into the mirror that she would want to hide away in a darkened room.

"Fever and rash will go tomorrow as suddenly as they visited her. Trust me. I'm familiar with the northern air and its ravages,"

I said, resolving to put an end to Corinne's distress. He was grateful for my reassurance. We resumed our conversation about literature, land management, the clichés of Accrington life, with as much agitation and pleasure as before, but there were lengthy pauses in which I stared into the cup and the tealeaves, in dread contemplation of the misery I had visited upon Corinne. Was I truly the cause of it? Did I have the ability (perhaps an inheritance from my mother) to curse, or was Corinne's illness pure coincidence? Terence abided these silences, thinking perhaps I was remembering my father, for I had recently told him (with greatly modified details) of his decay. When Terence rose to leave he hugged me and kissed my forehead shyly, his first physical contact with me.

"Your father will be fine. If I can help in any way don't hesitate to ask."

"You can paddle him one with an iron pipe to his head and finish him off for all I care," I wanted to reply, but the emotion on my face was reserved for Corinne's plight, and my possible part in it.

Corinne's rash and fever disappeared as I predicted. Her recovery caused me such relief that I repented of my hostility. Once more I admired her beauty, the luminosity of her presence. When I next encountered her I offered a weak smile even though she minced straight on, not acknowledging me. "She's fully concentrated over her studies," I told myself, surprised by my capacity for forgiveness. "She didn't ignore me. She's only worried about her essays." I paused a few yards after we passed each other. I pretended I had dropped something as an excuse to look back at her, to marvel at the swing of her hips, at her hair flowing like a sunlit rill. I resumed my journey, tilting and straightening, tilting and straightening, as if paying homage to earth, then to sky, me a creaking hinge between them, between life and afterlife. I suddenly saw my stick in a new light, pitying its condition. Once upon a time it was a green branch in the garden of the sun, giving shelter and free support to all manner of creatures, until hacked off, stripped, split and chiselled into an inert instrument. Once upon a time a flock of starlings soared from it towards the freedom of the sun. Now my dead weight bore down upon it, but it still gave free support, not discriminating between the winged and the earth-bound. A melancholy assailed me, an urgent wanting to cry, for I remembered the first time Dad's pals hacked and split and chiselled into me, and from the crevice they opened a flock of starlings arose as from the breached shelter of my body and flew away screaming.

*

My whiteness was the whiteness of a wood-louse, Corinne's of milk. I made every effort to protect her from future harm but failed. I was unable to suppress my desire to see her sour and curdle, becoming as repellent as my wood-louse appearance. After a month or so I sent another curse her way, to punish her for her pulchritude, a rash more severe than the first.

"It's come back," Terence said with such misery that I repented and recalled the curse.

"It's gone," he said when he next returned to my room. "In less than two days. I wonder whether Corinne has picked up a recurring germ?"

"It'll not come back," I reassured him.

The rash was banished but my compassion was soon breached and I gave her chicken-pox which incapacitated her for a week, and in November, to spoil her enjoyment of the Halloween party, a urinary taint. A mildly irritable one for I could not bring myself to replicate the burning and searing of my insides from the infections I picked up intermittently from Dad's pals.

"What's wrong with the poor thing this time?" I asked, and Terence muttered something about her passing bright yellow water.

"As bright as her hair is it?" I asked, pausing to dwell upon Corinne's blonde cascade. "Oh well, it'll soon go. All things passeth away, the good Lord says, even bright yellow urine. Let us two have some tea." I set off for the kitchen, leaving my stick behind. I walked out of my room slowly, pausing at the door, wanting him to admire my gait, for there was barely a wobble in my step. I returned bearing two mugs of tea, not a drop spilt. He was too shy to comment on my new-found straightness, and I was at a loss to explain it, so we didn't raise it as a subject of conversation. This was a great relief for how could I tell him that I believed my stability depended on Corinne's decline? That the more frail she became the more I could walk across the college grounds, never mind to the kitchen, without the aid of my stick? True, you couldn't say I could stride resolutely across the lawn, for there were still signs of dragging and hobbling, but all the same there was no stick and I reached the lecture hall in good breath.

"You're happy today, what's that you're humming?" he asked. I stopped stirring sugar into the mugs.

"Don't you know it? Honestly? We used to sing it all the time in school and Church. It's 'Jesus wants me for a sunbeam'. Silly really, at my age. It's a song more for children."

"You must have had a happy childhood, I bet," he said smiling kindly. "Go on, show us some photographs, do you have any?"

Photographs! Mention of the word made me laugh nervously.

"You must have a few amongst your belongings," he insisted, looking around the room.

"We never had photographs taken, except once."

"Once!"

"We're not like your lot down south with clean faces and clean features, so we don't bother. Except at weddings, but even then Mum didn't have one, so it's not that common."

"It's true, I have a dozen of me growing up, photography has taken off in a big way and it's got cheaper. What's the occasion you had your photograph done?"

"My Dad had a pal with a camera. He took it in our house."

"Have you got it on you?"

"No I haven't, and you wouldn't care to see it either. I wasn't looking my best…"

I was sitting on a chair, my legs spread apart and my body arched back to emphasise my breasts and to conceal my face. Copies of the photograph were supplied to the rest of the pals and to a wider circulation. There must have been a ready market for pictures of brazenly nude teenagers for Dad made quite a packet from my image. "Why didn't you show my face?" I complained to Dad when I saw the photograph. "I look like a headless carcass of a piglet hung up in the butcher's." "You look sweet sixteen," he said staring at the space between my thighs. "Next time I want to see myself or I'll not do it again," I sulked. "I can't show your face, only the rest of you, otherwise they'll jail me once the police recognise you," he explained, but I continued to sulk even though the rest of me was indeed pleasing to the eye.

"Shame you weren't looking your best," Terence sympathised.

"That's what I told Dad," I said.

*

"Jesus wants me for a sunbeam…" I had barely finished singing when Terence knocked on the door. I let him in and led him straight to bed. He followed meekly as if he had already anticipated an escalation of my tuition about northern ways. "Nowt about kidney soup and pig's bladder today," I told him, drawing the curtains to diminish the light. "Today's lesson is a woman's northern work. All day she feeds a shuttle with spools of cotton thread. When one spool is empty, she has to find the end of the thread of the new spool and suck it through a hole in the shuttle." I pressed him to the bed and unbuckled his belt. He made a faint attempt to resist but surrendered the moment he felt my tongue lapping at his nakedness. He stiffened, moaned, and in no time at all was spent. He began to apologise for the mess he had made on the sheets but I stopped his mouth with a hefty kiss.

Our future meetings together were shorn of conversation. He moved immediately to my bed where I undressed and performed for his delectation. The noise of his passion brought me to climax. There was a measure of reason in our unruliness. To begin with, I treated him gently, teasing and tempting him, letting him enter and bask within me, then withdrawing abruptly so that he was left in disarray and begged to be enveloped again. I was teaching him to crave, to become so demonic that he would kill to be satisfied. In later sessions I pawed at his nipples, I bit into the most tender parts of his flesh, arousing him to fury, addicting him to cries of pain and the sight of blood. Finally, I taught him how to beg to be beaten and subjugated, how to plead for this or that unspeakable act to be inflicted upon him. I taught him the pleasure of humiliation, the deadening of the self. I brought him to the brink of death and then I permitted him to ejaculate, to surge back into life, pressing my hand to his mouth to suppress the dark growling. I was expert at suffocating him, bringing him to within a breath of unconsciousness. I knew knots like any seasoned sailor. But it was not technique that tortured him, made beasts rear from his loins only to cower before me; it was the words I whispered in his ear, threats and fantasies which, as they became more and more graphic, made the noises in his throat sound uglier and uglier. There was a measure of reason in our unruliness, the movement from normal sex to adventuring into a supernatural realm.

I bestowed upon Terence the privileges I'd gained from the Accrington pals, those who had turned me into a urinal, and then sniffed at me; who rubbed dissolved lime into my mind, cleansing it of morality; who sat like toads between my thighs. He was gratified by my expertise, my physical and verbal rhapsodies, for Dad had brought me to perfection. There was no act of copulation that I had not already participated in or could not imagine and speak vividly. By the age of sixteen I was already a veteran, a widespread mistress. Such talent gave me confidence, it propped me up more securely than my stick. I only lapsed when I caught sight of creatures like Corinne, whose beauty and innocence reminded me of a little girl playing at being a greengrocer's assistant, selling oranges and pears; a little girl jolted into frightful knowledge by the screaming of a bird. I cursed my mother for abandoning me to the terror of the bird when she should have cupped my heart in her hands, keeping it safely until I could give it over romantically to someone like Terence. Instead I fed Terence the bile of my self-loathing, squatting over him in the posture of the Moor that was my father.

I resolved once again to be kind to Corinne, but soon surrendered to jealousy with the same unpleasantness as I had surrendered to Dad and his squad. I sent her a new condition, an eating disorder to wither her frame, to turn her into the image of Mum in her final years. Terence didn't care for Corinne as before. When he came to my room there was only a trace of concern on his face, which vanished as soon as I stripped and played with him in Accrington ways, with iron and fire and catastrophe. I played at being a red-hot poker being dipped in his blood, making it hiss and steam; a cog loosening and flying off, the machinery shrieking to a halt; an underground explosion burying men under collapsed beams. He left my room maimed and gratified, returning the next day for more belittling, even as Corinne shrunk in sickness.

In the days I was indisposed he would still visit, as if to perfect his begging, for I would not permit him to enter me. I was blunt with him. "I don't want blood all over the sheets."

"I'll pay for a new set, a new bed even! Please, Molly."

"Keep your money for a whore or a wife," I scolded him. They always offered to pay, the rich! His mention of money was not a sign of his debasement, merely recourse to the natural behaviour of his class.

He begged rear entry, or to be placated in my mouth, but I stood my ground firmly. "What can I give to sway you?" he pleaded.

"Give me Corinne." The words came automatically, spoken by a presence within me that was unfamiliar to me.

"What do you mean 'give me Corinne'?" His face trembled with excitement. He was imagining me stroking Corinne's thighs in small circular motions, demarcating the space to be daubed by my tongue. He was imagining me staring at its golden down and tendrils of light before tasting. I had read somewhere that Raleigh, shown a nugget of gold supposedly brought back from Demerara, gazed upon it, then put it in his mouth and sucked on it, satisfying himself of its reality. He sucked on it, then bit upon it, fearful that it would crumble and dissolve into insubstantiality. When it remained solid, he groaned in delight, wanting to swallow the nugget, to embellish his stomach, to keep it a secret within. Not out of greed, but in gratitude for the benediction of something more solid than flesh. At the time I didn't appreciate Raleigh's delirium but Terence's mood made me understand it, though partially. An explorer, Terence had become addicted to the quest for greater and greater peril. He was testing the limits of his flesh, wanting to venture beyond conscience and a sense of mortality. Like Dad's pals he wanted to hack away at me, clearing ground of rules of class, religion, family, to arrive at… what? There was no word for it, the thrill of discovery was as unspeakable as the thing discovered, but I intuited it had to do with a realm beyond death, beyond the predictable stages of flesh's decay. "Give me Corinne," I said, but he misunderstood me, imagining that I wanted to take her through and beyond the ordeals of debauchery, to a supernatural realm, but I was claiming her for death. Only for death, for I believed in nothing else. Nothing survived. The shapes that appeared in Mum's crystal ball were illusions or fabrications, or reflections of her own mortal face.

"What do you want of Corinne?" he asked eventually, and in a debauched whisper.

The voice that issued from me was as strange as any of the voices that spoke through Mum in her state of possession, and although I didn't recognise it, I knew it belonged to me. "Put out the light and then put out the light of her," I said, then paused to come to terms with the iniquity of my confession.

Terence nodded vigorously. "I will, I will," he said, hoping that his assent would gain him my favours. I looked upon his nakedness, the cruelty of it, the tumescence aimed in my direction like a cannon. "What will you do?" I asked, mocking his ignorance. "Will you kill her for me, is that what I seek from you?"

He blinked stupidly, attentive only to his craving, perhaps thinking that I was asking him to re-enact our death-games upon Corinne's body, for death-games had been the culmination of our love-making, me garrotting him with a make-believe cord whilst whispering obscenities in his ear, tightening and tightening until he heaved and spewed forth his life like a cannon firing into nothingness, for the sake of nothingness. But death-games were not what I was asking of him, for in spite of Corinne's emaciation, I wanted to doubt that I wielded any real or imaginary power over her. My curses were wishful thinking, Corinne's various sicknesses were hers, I insisted to myself. I merely wanted her to go away, to stop haunting my mind. She appeared to me in a rush of light such as angels announced their presence. The same rush of light that blinded me when Mum prodded the bomb or when Dad poked within me. "I don't want the light, I don't want the light," I blurted out. "From the time I was little that's all I've ever had." I looked away from Terence, tired of his incomprehension, his callowness. For all the initiations into an unclean carnality, he remained white. The milkyness of an eighteen year old. The whiteness of an angel's wings. I looked away from Terence to witness my own craving. I loosened the garrotte from my mind, and a series of images gushed forth. The enamel bath. The painted mansion set in lawns and flower gardens. The cantering of white steeds. The sheen of knightly weaponry. The sizzle and flare from the mouth of cannonry. Mum's dead eyes polished to the condition of her crystal ball. Dad and his pals like blowtorches within me. Stars. No, none of these I wanted. Let me be rid of these. Let me not be seen. Let me scuttle away to the comfort of shadows.

"I want a child," the voice within me addressed Terence, though my face was still turned away from him.

"A child?" In the long silence that followed I could hear his blood pitching in panic. Laughter broke from me and when it ceased tears came with such strength that I thought they would wash away my eyes.

For the whole of the next week I hid indoors, seeking comfort in shadow and oblivion. I drew the curtains, kept the electric light switched off, refused to heed Terence knocking on my door. The memories will go, I told myself, squeezing into the darkest corner of the room, drawing up my feet to my chest to reduce my visibility. In the hours after Dad's first breaching of me I had curled up on myself thus. So too after the initiation with his pals, but the child in me had gone forever. I would always be seen. To pretend otherwise was deception, and when I eventually came to the realisation of this, I slackened, I opened myself, I squealed for the pals like a sow pleasuring in mud.

The week passed, the memories remained, the most insistent of which were the ways I'd open and unfold, ovulate with glee, daring Dad and the pals to bolder explorations. I was fearless of light, I stretched and radiated, exposing every pool, inlet and channel. To pretend that I was other than gratified was deception, though when they left I felt only a longing, and unfulfilment, as if my insides had been drained and only stone ground remained. I waited for the next night and the next, to be irrigated, drained, irrigated again.

The week passed, I arose and made an attempt to resume my study. Hiding from the world was useless, I would never regain invisibility. I was cast into the light of revelation but it was not too late for Terence and Corinne to recover their sheltered selves. It had to be lifted, my corruption of Terence, of Corinne. I had bewitched both of them, but my conscience began to weigh down upon me, and the power I may have wielded over them became a burden I could no longer carry. My hip suffered. I was walking across campus with renewed limp, more than ever dependent on my stick. Once more I admitted Terence to my bed, but there was no longer a relishing of his body. It was no longer pristine, it held no allure. He had turned into swine. He smelt of my father's sweat. My task was to convert him back to his innocent self, to restore Corinne to health, to a brightness that was different to the light of accusation I shone upon myself.

The chance came with the letter from a neighbour telling of my father's rapid decline, urging me to return to his death-bed. When Terence appeared that afternoon I was prepared as usual, the sheets freshly spread, my body bathed and perfumed, my eyelashes and make-up in place. He went straight to bed, undressed, sprawled. There was sorrow in my eyes. I looked at his body, the youthfulness of it, and I remembered our first moments of intimacy, how scented in newness his flesh was, for it had not yet sloughed off its adolescence. I wiped away the tears and saw him clearly, saw the twitching and impatience of one addicted to perversion. "I'll not come to bed, I have something to tell," I said, refusing his demand.

And I told him all.

*

Terence was dumbstruck, then the questioning and the doubt. Yes, I vomited the first time, but the pals wiped the sides of my mouth, tenderly, as if re-enacting their first deeds of fatherhood. They cradled me in their arms, wiping the sides of my mouth, trying to remember a long forgotten lullaby, trying to tune their aged and broken voices to a song for the new. They cradled me, crooned over me, comforted me, I told Terence. Yes, after a while I willingly played child to their imagining of past love, past fatherhood. I was a bright coin in their lap, reflecting the gleam in their eyes. It was my father who debased me, broke the circle of fascination. He pocketed the coin, spent it on tobacco and backstreet doctors. Yes, I had three or four abortions before I grew barren. And there were all manner of home-made remedies for the various ailments, the acid urination, the swollen glands.

And your mother? And your neighbours? And your school-teachers? Did no-one inform the police? Terence stuttered out his questions, and I held up my hands to quell his doubt, but he who only sought out my sex, hammering his lust into me, could not now see the memory of nails appearing miraculously in the palms of my hands. He had dug into my orifices, but when he had finished they had closed over and recovered and become whole, with the slow elasticity of a slug. Holes appeared instead in my hands, phantom holes, but being callow he could not intuit them.

I reached for my stick and hobbled out of the room, wanting to look back one last time to savour his nakedness. I imagined he would giggle when my back was turned, nervous by my confession, appalled by his association with me. He was bound to bend over the bed and retch, as I did the first time. Let him close his eyes in horror, let images of suicide haunt him, for Corinne will tend to him, she will cradle him in the light of her arms, soothe his torment with song, that when he awakens to the shimmer of her love all memory of me will be eclipsed.

"Don't look back, don't act the jilted lover," I told myself. But I did look back, exposing the shame streaking my face like tears, dislodging my careful make-up. Fool! Fool! I must have blinked too hard or tensed my face in an effort to conceal my feelings, for an eyelash slipped its fastening and fell upon my jumper. I tried to brush it off but it was caught in the wool. It lay there like an unwanted thing, curled up in vulnerability to my anger, all its tiny desperate fingers clinging to my chest. A spider of self-loathing curled comically, lovingly at my chest, refusing to be brushed off.

I closed the door behind me, imagining his giggling, his voiding of his stomach. Perhaps he was not crying sordidly, perhaps he was calling, calling me back in an urge to forgive. "You were innocent, you were seduced into their sick rich ways," he wanted to tell me. "Come back to me my language, my know-ledge of the world," he was saying, promising to restore a scrubber like me to my enamelled self, polishing me with chivalrous words, with cloth scented in the air of foreign climes.

Whatever his reaction I closed the door and headed to the station, passing the lecture theatre on my way. Corinne was at the entrance talking to her friends. She was skinnier than usual but just as diaphanous, her skin stretched over bone as if to catch whatever light fell upon the city. She resembled a child wrapped in the airiness of malnutrition, but she had painted her fingernails red as if to assert her substantial self. The life which I had tried to extinguish had drained into her fingertips, dyeing the nails red. I had lost control of her as I had of Terence. Suddenly, she stopped speaking, turned and stared at me. I lowered my eyes instantly, for if I did not I knew I would be dazzled by her look which threatened to give her sovereignty over my crippled state.

From that moment I learnt never to raise my eyes to what lay beyond my conception of a crippled state. When Corinne looked upon me she restored to me my ordinariness. The Virgin looked upon the peasant whom I recognised as myself. Mum would peer into things to reveal their ancient worth, but Mum lied. Corinne was the light of truth – the truth that I had no calling, nothing special. Corinne, whom I had tried to reduce to a child, had become my true mother.

*

Dad was dead before I could reach him. He looked so nondescript, lacking in worth, needless of greeting. The welfare people and the undertaker had got him laid out in the front room awaiting my return. It was an unvarnished coffin, made from leftover planks of wood, and instead of gleaming copper handles there were pieces of rope. Joseph Countryman would have done a better job. When I looked at my Dad in his cheap carriage I felt grief, not for my mother who had spent her honeymoon nights in the same parlour on a borrowed mattress, for there had been no money as yet to acquire a bed and furniture; not for myself, who was milked by my father for a regular nightly income. I felt grief for Joseph Countryman who had fashioned doors and cupboards with such care, a man in love with the subtlety of his chisel, who over the years had drawn in so much wood-dust into his lungs that his breath was always redolent of pine; Joseph Countryman who stood on a chair he had recently made (with emblematic beasts of the forest carved along its back and legs), and roped a ceiling beam. He shoved the chair away with a tender kick, careful not to bruise it, like a mother playing with its cub, pawing it, boxing its face, handling it in mock roughness, preparing it for a future as painful and brutish and lonely as a rope tightening against windpipe. Dad's going, a century later, was a disappointment compared to the circumstance of Joseph Countryman's suicide. I wept for both of them, for the stench of Dad's life and for the stretched neck of the carpenter.

The slow changing of the seasons, months bleeding into months, but I remained in Accrington in the solitude of an orphan and a widow. The rent accumulated thickly, I hid from the landlord and ate scraps off dirty plates. One night there was a ringing of the doorbell. Normally I ignored all the attempts of the neighbours to support me, refusing their sympathy by keeping the door locked. This time I answered it on impulse, alerted to a strange encounter. An elderly woman was there, the grey strands of her hair pasted to her head because of the rain. "Come in from the wet," I said, reaching for her hand but she withdrew and shivered at the prospect of my touch. She stood there in her soaking dress, her eyes widened as she looked me up and down. There was a sudden gust of wind, and the rattling of old window frames all along the street. The rain fell steadily. "It'll be chundering in a second, don't linger at the door," I said, but she would not budge from surveying me with shining eyes. Soon after I spoke, as if summoned by my voice, a huge thunderclap breached the sky and the rain pelted down. I closed the door instinctively, then remembering my manners, opened it again to the old woman who was in the same spot, seemingly numb to the lashing of the rain. Her eyes were fixed on me with the same glaring intensity. She was a tattered scarecrow, her head of straw in a state of sogginess, her dress soiled by bird-dung, but with jewels stitched into her eye sockets which would not loosen or dim in spite of the weather. "Come in, come in, I won't harm you, I'm Molly, I live here on my own," I said, anxious to avoid the appearance of lightning, its reflection in her occult eyes.

"I know who you are," she said in a neutral tone of voice, neither alert with emotion nor insensibly dull. I recognised it instantly as the voice that issued from my mother when she raised her head from the crystal ball to communicate between the living and the dead. I panicked, I went to close the door but my hands were frozen in the darkness of the sky. The sky, tufts of dark clouds, sheep frozen in a dreamless sleep. I waited sheepishly at the open door while she addressed me, calling my name over the noise of the rain. "Molly. I know you. I am watching you this very moment. I can see all of you, every curve and straight line, I know the whole alphabet and notation of your body, I can read your mind."

"Who are you? What do you want?" I stammered, wanting to shut her from sight, return to the seclusion of the house, but my hands were immobile.

"I am Harold, the one with the eye patch and a pocketful of pounds. As if you can forget your Harold! Harold the banker who saved your Dad from conscription and now has come to save you too. I've come to squint at you one last time, my wife will give you the money, I'll not send her again to distress you." She stopped speaking, reached into her pocket and handed me a package, soiled and wet. My hands were aroused, they reached for the package. "Leave me alone," I sobbed, wanting to drop it, but it remained steadfast in my hands. Grief formed like a furnace in my throat, I heard myself crying above the rain and the rattling pains and the crashing roof plates. The rain dropped thickly into my open mouth as if to dampen and put out the flames, but I spat it out, spat it out, spat it out, and all the time I was howling above the noise of the storm, howling to be left alone.

I cannot remember re-entering the house, or what happened to the old woman. Like a sheep I found my way instinctively through the storm to my place of refuge. A sheep, that's what I was, not the Lamb of God, as I used to believe when the pals left and I was filled with self-pity; the Lamb of God offered up as sacrifice to fill their nostrils and bellies and loins with the scent and tender meat of the Holy. Not the Lamb of God, nor the fledgling bird fallen from its nest and trust and tree, screaming at the crouched cat. I used to think too of myself as a slug, stretching and withdrawing, moist, fleshy, arousingly elastic, but the slug left a silver trail behind it. For all its obscene appearance it was precious within, issuing silver from its belly, whilst mine was barren. Not the Lamb of God nor the fledgling bird nor slug, but a sheep, a black sheep, black as a sky tufted with rain clouds, frozen in dreamless sleep. A sheep ambling from this pastured loin to the other, then back to its pen, insensible of wrongdoing. Dad had turned me into a passive stupid creature, singular in appetite, settled in its routine and habit.

I recovered as abruptly as Mum would, raising her eyes from her crystal ball, shaking her head, letting out a huge wheeze of breath then drawing in deeply, the fresh draught of air bringing her back from the theatre of the dead. I opened Harold's package to find a wad of bank notes wrapped in a letter. "Harold here," it opened chirpily and continued in the same light-hearted tone. "I'll be dead by the time you read this. Somewhere in dodoland. Dropped off, pegged out, hopped the twig, but I'm still twittering for you. I know I didn't do too good by you when I was Accrington – alive – but here's some money. Fly not too far from me, little chick. I'll watch over you through my wife's eyes, she is as receptive to me as always. Fifty years of marriage to her meant we became one, she looked in the mirror and saw me, when she walked the streets it was my voice she heard in her head. Which is why I took delight in you, for I was bored with her as my familiar, I was bored talking to her in her head and she talking in mine. You were new, unspoken, not spoken for. I came to you because I wanted to hear you sounding like a pup and craving for the nipple of me. You know the sounds – the little gasp, the whimper, the baby gurgle and cry. So rejuvenating after the daily dull conversations with my wife. I love you for stirring my old roots, so take the money, your nest-egg, go to Coventry, it's cheap to live, a lovely spot from all accounts, rebuilding going on, a place for the future. I know because they opened up a new branch of the bank there. Deposit the money in Coventry, it'll grow rapidly, you'll thank me."

I tore the letter in two, then tore it again and again, trying to reduce it into pieces so tiny that it would disappear from sight. I gathered them up and went to light a fire, to throw them into it, but there was no coal in the house. In a fit of panic I mashed the pieces into a ball and swallowed it, my tongue wiping and scouring my gum and teeth to make sure nothing remained behind. I sat down, contented that I had finished him off once and for all, but the bank notes sat on the table, the King's eyes (and behind them, Harold's) staring smugly at me. I would get rid of the money, but I knew I would remain destitute, and the realisation that I was still wedded to Harold's need of me filled my stomach with nausea. I vomited involuntarily for the hundredth and more time in my life, but the letter was lodged within me. I thrust my fingers in my throat, but he remained steadfast in his love, like an infant wilfully fastened to his mother's nipple, even in her state of mummification.

I packed a small bag, a few items of clothing for myself, the rest a sample of Dad's belongings – his pipe, tobacco tin, cap, belt – and took the first train south, getting off, after an hour, at a place called Sunbury. I found a room in a boarding house and stayed there for three days in total seclusion, neither eating nor washing, with the blinds drawn. I set off for the station, took another train, disembarking at Creston, five miles away. South, always south to my mother's green dream, to Terence's habitation, but first the necessary purging of the past by living in isolated rooms, starving myself, letting my hair grow unruly, letting dirt encase my body, feeding flakes of dead skin to bed mites. I voyaged from boarding house to boarding house, edging my way south. People made a space for me on the trains, for I smelt badly, and landladies shut their doors in my face except when I held out one of Harold's bank notes. The war may have ended but there was still misery everywhere, so landladies took the money and let into their houses the unclean creature I had become. Three weeks of wandering and rented rooms, fasting and gathering dirt to my solitary self, my only companion my stick, faithful as ever, but still I should not have been surprised when it began to complain. The first time it did so I chided it and it fell silent. "Remember your place, stick," I said, and the human authority of my voice stilled it that night and all the next day, though it sulked, giving off an unpleasant smell of resin, reminding me of the childhood tree I climbed to save the fledgling. We were in a women's hostel in Bentham, one hundred and three miles', fourteen days or more, journeying to Terence's village (I would travel no more than five or six miles a day, giving myself enough time for the self-chastisement necessary before I could encounter him) and it was incumbent upon my stick, my steed, to take me there safely with the gifts I was carrying for Terence, my father's pipe, tobacco tin, cap and belt. Hence my sternness when the stick first attempted a complaint, but I could not rein it in for long. Late the next afternoon, in the midst of my rehearsal of the words with which I would greet Terence, it slipped from its place against the wall and fell to the floor. Weak as I was I still got out of bed to lean it against the wall, and though my tongue was a withered toad in my mouth I spoke gentle words to it. "Not far from now my faithful steed, my Phaeton," I said, stroking the curve of its neck. "Soon we'll arrive, and then I'll free you to roam in the forest beside Terence's village, I'll not need you then, I'll no longer burden you with my dead weight, for Terence will touch my waist, take away the palsy, and I will rise from my pallet and walk again with gracious posture." I turned to go back to bed but before I reached it fell to the floor again.

"You're no more than a fond and hopelessly failed woman," Stick said, in a whisper, for it was afraid to invoke my wrath. I was more stunned than angry. I sat in a daze on my bed, and my obvious frailty encouraged it to continue its arraignment, but in a tone more of pity than of recrimination.

"I have done you fealty and due observance, ten years and more have passed since you first summoned me to service–"

"Oh my Puck and my delight, I'll free your spirit soon," I interrupted, filled with gratitude and yet guilt for I had neither heeded its voice nor sought its counsel before. "I have taken insufficient care of thee, pet, but you must forgive me, for I am foolish as you say, though not yet fourscore in age." It relented, for when it spoke again it was in a softened tone.

"In my various lives I have witnessed marvels and terrors but never such a piteous creature such as thou art."

I stifled a sob, urging it to continue, and it launched into a speech, part oration, part harangue, sesquipedalian and blunt in turns, mannered and crabbed. It began telling of itself as a branch of a spacious tree beneath which medieval lovers met in green innocence. Birds, harvest, maidens bathing in a nearby stream, pageants and merriments that announced the changing of the seasons – such scenes marked the centuries it witnessed.

"Oh Stick, why do you speak dross to me? I am not sentimental like my mother, she who believed in knights and what-not!"

Stick resented my interruption but all the same surrendered to my desire for bleaker confession. "To be true, the idyll was shattered one day by a rope flung around a fork, at the end of which a man was hoisted and dropped, a Royalist – you could tell from his robes and gentle frame – whilst Cromwell's men, sturdy, ruddy, flat-footed yeomen, cheered at his execution." I listened attentively as Stick described a line of prisoners, each waiting his turn to be hung, some stern-faced at their fate, as if certain of their divine cause, others a pulp of fear, pleading for mercy. The next day and the next, and for weeks afterwards, lines of new prisoners and their gleeful executioners. The idyll of the forest was forever destroyed. Stick jumped centuries to the late Victorian period, the surrounding land long parcelled into factory plots and tenements for the slum people, but the tree to which it belonged was now in the garden of a mill-owner. A swing hung from it and giggly children in pretty frocks were pushed to and fro by a nurse. Then the time came for the tree to be cut down, to make way for a car-port, and the useful parts of it sent to a local manufacturer who fashioned tables and chairs from it, and rods for various purposes, one of which eventually came into my ownership and was now divulging its biography.

"I tell you the English side of me, but my forebears were from Muslim lands. One branch of the family tree beheld crusaders engaging with Saladin at the Battle of Jerusalem." Stick paused to allow me to take in its distinguished and ancient pedigree. "Some crusaders brought back to England seeds and cuttings from the East, which they grew and mated with local species, so my sap is the splendour of merged continents, at once Muslim and Christian."

"Alas, I am native Accrington, as common as a coal-seam," I said, deliberately modest so as to feed its own pride. "And what of the other sticks made from the tree, your brothers and sisters?" I asked, prodding it into happy confession.

"Oh, we are as catholic as the world is. We have become Bishops' staffs, or rods of chastisement, or we prop up the status quo, or we conduct symphonies, or we beat back bushes to recover shot pheasants. One of us even found itself in the hand of Field Marshal Rommel, in Africa, gilded and ornamented as befits a great soldier's baton. How horrible when it had to beat a hasty retreat across the African desert towards Berlin! But you distract me, for you are my true subject, though I am your servant and pedicle."

"Hush! Speak not of me but of others, tell me again of all the men and women who have rested in your shade or passed you by on their way to foreign adventures."

It refused, however, to be waylaid, guiding me through darkness back to myself as the blind are led to certain destination. "In my various lives I have witnessed marvels and terrors but never such a piteous creature such as thou art. Once upon a time, when polio struck the land I was in constant favour and use, I gave succour to the needy, but their agony was naught compared to your predicament. Yours is an inward malady and blight of soul. Serum, transfusions, new medicines, deodorants, insect repellents, changes in hygiene, all these stay or even cure diseases but only prayer can ease yours. Come, kneel beside me, open your heart to Christ our Saviour and to Allah for They truly know the shame and the pain of males."

*

I woke up with two faces hovering above me, their eyes lit with alarm. "It's alright dear, we're here, you're in safe hands." I recognised the voice to be my landlady's.

"How long has she been in this state?" the man beside her asked.

"Five days she's been lodging here, quiet as a mouse until today, I heard babbling, and then screaming, then a crash, I thought she'd fallen down and sure enough when I came into her room she was a heap on the floor. I lifted her onto her bed, then called you, she looked right dead and colding rapidly."

"Is that you Terence?" I asked, reaching to touch the man's face but he withdrew and turned away.

"She does reek to high heaven, I'll have to use up two carbolics to purge myself of her smell," the landlady said. The man rifled through his bag. When he turned to me again he was wearing a mask.

"Don't scorn me Terence, and don't hide from me," I said, raising my hand again to fondle his face but he brushed it away. "I soiled you and I made Corinne sick, but I'm changed now. It was Dad who caused everything but I've cleansed myself of him, he's dead, all that's left of him are some bits and bobs which are in my bag, locked away so he can't break out like a rash and epidemic." I wanted to reassure Terence but he stood apart from me. I raised my body from the bed, seeking to be closer to him, to draw his head to my breasts, stroke and kiss his brow, rummage through his golden hair and wonder at my pirate's fortune. "I will plunder the treasury of your youth, and in the darkness of my unworthy self I will hold up each goblet, each gemstone and jewelled orb, and I will wonder at their glow."

"There, she's blabbing again," the housekeeper said. "She's scaring me, can't you do something for her, doctor, and be quick about it?"

I raised my voice above her fluttering and continued to address my Terence. "Then I will give back all the ornaments to you, their opulence increased, for now they bear the sheen of my astonishment. Nothing will I rob from my darling Terence which I will not return in greater splendour. The gift of your youth I seize, I possess, but then I give it back with its value increased because of the way I marvelled at it."

"Who's she talking to doctor? Aren't you going to give her an injection? I want her out of this house as soon as she's made decent."

"Hush woman," the man chided, irritated at the housekeeper's panic. "Keep watch over her whilst I call an ambulance. Where's your telephone?"

"Are you going to fetch me a carriage, Terence?" I called after him in a coy voice. "Will you marry me in the shadow of a cathedral? That's my secret longing, Terence, to marry you there. What a marvel and what a benediction to marry you in the shadow of a cathedral, in a space of forgiveness and renewal. I can see the coachmen, the carriages, the plumed horses, flowers flung upon us by our wedding party, and flashbulbs popping so rapidly that I have to rub my eyes to catch sight of your comeliness again. In my mind I see–" A snigger interrupted my vision. It was Stick. It was sniggering at me, making me the laughing stock of the wedding party and the world, but I would not surrender my dream of Terence to its cynicism. I retaliated in a barrage of accusations. "Stick, you're nothing but a Catholic and a Jacobite," I yelled, "and a lover of incense and bishops. And a traitor to your country, lauding Rommel. And you're impure, you've got a bit of Saladin in you. And Harold the Jew once owned you, gave you to me. Worst of all you're an assassin of birds, those beautiful pheasants which you beat back the bush to find shot and dying. Oh Stick, you are my assassin, what am I but a bird terrorised and robbed of its innocent life?"

The housekeeper ran from the room, shouting at the top of her voice, "Doctor, doctor, hurry, she's gone completely nuts, she'll kill us all."

An ambulance was called to take me away, but before it could arrive I grabbed my bag of Harold's bank notes and hurried from the house. I would escape Stick and take a train further south, out of earshot of its insults. The Nazi! The Mohammedan! The Jacobite! I punctuated my walk by cursing Stick thus, each curse keeping me upright so that I was able to make my way steadily towards the station. The high street was a sea of shoppers which parted at my approach, and I cursed them as I passed through, calling them Moors, child-molesters, sacrificers, pyramid-fraudsters, grave-robbers. "Zion! Zion! Glory be to Heaven, I'm off to Zion," I announced at the top of my voice. I pursed my lips and blew an imagined Salvation Army trumpet, then I burst into a hymn, addressed to Terence, not the usual stale 'Jesus wants me for a Sunbeam' but a love-song of my own making, issuing from the mystery of me: "Glory to the lark arising / Glory to the weightless cloud / …" I floated through the crowd, independent of my feet, but the joy of the freed slave was not to last. I sang to hollow out myself, cast off memory and become weightless, but even as I sang the demons of the past which I had scattered began to recover, to regroup, to cling to my ankles. I slowed, then stopped in abrupt fright of myself. I found myself at the entrance of the local cinema, its poster advertising *The Return of the Money* though when I looked again it said *The Return of the Mummy*. The picture was of the gaunt face of Boris Karloff looming above a female with her winding sheet undone, revealing herself as a thing blackened and withered. She stared at me through sealed eyes, recognising me as kith and kin. I tried to look away but the urge to acknowledge her overcame me. "You are the only family left to me, my ugliness," I found myself saying to her, to comfort her in her state of sad exposure. The demons played at my feet, massaging my soles, reaching for my legs and thighs, coaxing me to accept ugliness as a thrill and a virtue. I could not summon strength to kick them away, my limbs were as immobilised as the mummy's. I stood beside the cinema poster unable to step away, and speechless, for when I tried to call Terence's name only mist plumed from my mouth.

It was in such a situation of helplessness that Stick found me. I heard a sudden commotion behind me, and when I turned round there was Stick tap-tap-tapping its way along the high street, resolutely ignoring the screaming and confusion of the crowd. Stick walked with the sure-footed swagger of a son of Saladin. When it reached me it paused to recover its breath and when it had done so and its heartbeat had settled, it leant towards me, seeking my hand. "Come with me, dearest mistress and bride," it said in a manly pagan voice, and without waiting for a response to its proposal it led me back to my chamber and bed.

*

It was thus that Stick and I plighted troth to each other, it was thus that we sought to be inseparable, I tried explaining to the psychiatrist, but all he did was to smile benignly at me. The nurses, too, listened to me with condescending attitude. I could not elicit a proper response from them. As if being wife to a stick was only a mildly uncommon state of matrimony. I should have eloped with a veritable Negro, that would have got them going, I told Stick, goading it to jealousy. "One such braced himself upon my cousin-rod," Stick replied, drifting into reverie. "A Negro of noble mien who bore himself with the dignity of his race. He wore a turban decorated with peacock feathers and his body was scented in the powders of Arabia…" Stick paused and sniffed the air. Its eyes misted over at the recollection of its cousin-stick which the Moor had carved into exotic shape and studded with pearls.

"Poor cousin, to be in the clutch of pagan hands," I said, wanting to deflate Stick, but it easily dismissed my effort, launching into a counter-attack.

"My cousin was wrested from the hands of a crusader at the height of battle. My cousin was originally fashioned into a plain cross, but the victorious Moor remade it into a glorious staff and symbol of his nobility. And look at me, the least of our family, a thing of degraded status, the lover of a lewd cripple and lunatic…" It sighed, and with such despair that I instantly forgave its insult.

"I'm sorry that you've ended up with a carbuncle such as I am," I said, striving to apologise and yet retain my dignity. "I admit to being a malignancy, a malediction. Call me minacious, call me miscreant, call me a slubberdegullion–"

"Cut the crap, you know you're just a used-up cunt."

Its bluntness was a blow to my head. It took me a while to recover. "You're right, that's all I have become, a gash and an opening caked in dirt," I said. "You must leave me, I am unworthy of your attention. I have never known love, and never will. Have you known love, dearest Stick?"

My question quelled its anger; it drifted into reverie again. "Only when I was part of a tree, not since I was chopped and made stick-shape." And it told me of the time when it was a branch, of a red squirrel brushing her tail against it. It told me of a woodpecker piercing its heart day after day. I lay in bed beside it, not touching, sullen in jealousy as it disclosed a sylvan past.

We quarrelled, we were reconciled, and the days passed in wondrous talk. It had seen much more of the world than me, and over a period of centuries. It took pride in revealing itself as a stick of many languages, showing off its refinement by punctuating its speech with medieval Italian or Renaissance English. "…*E per la mesta selva saranno*… Through the dismal wood our bodies will be hung…" When I looked puzzled it would lean towards me and whisper conspiratorially, "Dante, from Canto XIII, amazing stuff, read it for yourself, suicides' souls trapped in trees. Dante's a far superior poet to Terence." On the subject of the divine rights of Kings, antique words would tumble forth from its mouth like drunkards emerging from an Elizabethan tavern. It spoke of the discovery of El Dorado in Demerara, of Cortez, of Inca temples. I expressed amazement, which pleased it. Whenever a point of contention arose I placated it by demurring to its superior knowledge of things. Stick was braggadocio and self-elation, I was fluff and flattery. I grew to resent it. Our relationship had reverted to one similar to Dad and his pals, me a serving-girl to their male puff. I wished I could suffer like the other patients in the wards. Their suffering was uncomplicated compared to mine. All of them heard voices, but none so irritating, so supercilious, as Stick's. There was one called Peter, a young boy orphaned in a car accident, brain damaged, robbed of speech. His parents were harmless enough in their aftercare of him. "Change your shirt," his dead mother would chide. "Stop biting your nails," his dead father said. Peter scowled but in the end he was an obedient son, brushing his teeth before going to sleep, folding away his clothes, but in particular (and without prompting from his parents) polishing his shoes and placing them, laces neatly tied, at the foot of the bed. Stick took an instant dislike to him, no doubt sensing my fondness for the boy. "What a silly thing," it opined. "Why all the attention to his shoes, it's not as if he's going anywhere!'

"He's already been, to heaven and back," I retorted. Stick harrumphed then gave me one of its scornful looks, as if to say "sillier bitch you". I could have explained to Stick that Peter had walked with Jesus as his faithful disciple, I could have quoted chapter and verse from Holy Scripture telling how Jesus especially washed Peter's feet at the Last Supper, or of Peter healing a lame man outside the temple in Jerusalem, but Stick would have been deaf to the Gospels. It had regressed into memory of the glory of infidel Turks, it revelled in the repulse of the crusaders. I was loath to open up ancient theological disputation in case we both lost our temper, our commotion stirring the other patients to strife and the psychiatrist ordering me to be strait-jacketed.

"It's to do with the mystery of feet," I said decisively, but Stick would not let the matter rest.

"You're a cripple, that's why you're obsessed by feet," it goaded me. I acquiesced to keep the peace, once more subjecting myself to its male arrogance, but all the same quietly deciding to befriend Peter.

Each morning I went to the boy, awakening him by stroking his face, and, in full view of Stick, kissing his forehead. Peter opened his eyes and looked deeply into me, so deeply that my body trembled. Eventually I mumbled something or the other and he smiled at my confusion. I knew then the troubled soul and arousal when Jesus called upon the disciples. "Follow me, I will make you a fisherman of souls," Jesus had said and Peter put aside his net and stepped unsteadily from his boat, falling headlong into the water, knowing that he was being summoned to his death and immortality. Peter took one last look at the fish caught in his net, lashing and suffocating, yet in the throes of painful death lit by the morning sun and by the radiance of the divine. Stick, suddenly all Muslim and deaf to the Gospels, was also blind to the light pouring through the hospital window onto the boy's face and the disciple's soul. For all its display of erudition, it was an insensitive thing, and I resolved to put it away forever, to walk by my own strength and in stumbling doubt towards the calling of Our Lord. Stick sneered, reminding me of my useless hip, and Peter's parents raised alarmed voices against me, instructing the boy not to pay heed to my gesture of love. "She's fake, she's sinner, she's succulent, she'll debauch you," they screamed at Peter. "Cast her out, she's not your kind," they cried but Peter lay in bed warming to the morning light and to my stroking of his forehead, gazing so deeply into me that the darkness of my womb lifted, revealing neither bruising nor the suppuration of demons, but a nest freshly prepared for new birth, a second coming.

*

I took Peter into my care. I offered him a breast but as I was hoisting his mouth to it, Matron approached and slapped my hand away. "Get a hold of yourself," she shouted, shoving me back to my bed space. "If I catch you being vulgar again the doctor will do something drastic to you."

"Oh Matron, forgive me, Peter is indeed too old to be suckled. My error was genuine for I have no experience of these matters. But please, teach me other ways to mother him, I beg of you, Matron."

Stick burst out laughing. "You're a nutcase, that's what you are. Imagine thinking you can mother anybody, a heap of northern spite like you. Mothers have moistness in them, mothers are scented like medlars…"

"But I can learn, I can learn how to be tender, just tell me how, O sage one."

Stick was momentarily flattered, but the urge to chastise me returned. "The closest you'll come to being a mummy is as an Egyptian ghoul," it said. It was as if its words were the movement of a magician's wand for the hag appeared on cue, the hag who was Harold's wife. She materialised from thin air, soaked to the skin like before. "Are you still caught in the same storm, can't you escape the mockery of lightning?" I asked her. I wanted to dry her hair, comb out its knots and wrap her face in a black warm cloth. But Harold would not allow blind tenderness between us. "Get thee yonder to Coventry," he growled from her throat. Mention of Coventry opened in my mind the spectacle of a new Jerusalem, a city rising from the rubble of barbarian destruction. "Coventry, Coventry," Harold repeated, but the more he insisted, the more I was determined to turn my eyes away from the image of promise he evoked: the new Coventry branch of his bank. Doubt mixed with spite and brought song to my tongue. "Men and money / buying honey / men and money / growing runny / twix' the legs / making dregs." And when I finished singing I squared up to Harold's wife with such determination that she backed off and had to sit on my bed to steady herself. "Tell your fiend-husband that I'll wallop him one, even though he's dead already. Tell your Harold that it was me who bashed my Dad over the head and sent him to hell to go and eat pig shit in the company of his mate Leviticus. I'm afraid of none, tell him that." But Harold would not be cowed. He called my bluff. He spoke again, this time not in words but in a cornucopia of metal. A shower of sovereigns, half-crowns, crowns, erupted from his wife's mouth, fell upon my head. The shower became a hailstorm, soon the hospital floor was awash with coins. Matron's face changed, no longer set in stone. Her mouth issued sounds of rapture as she lifted her apron to catch the money. The patients – previously in various stages of coma – joined her, jumping from their beds to scoop up whatever fortune they could and stuff it under their pillows for safe-keeping. The coins continued to cascade and the once silent ward became a scene of shrieks and ululations. People became proper lunatics for they tore at each other, trampled upon each other, in their desperation for the money. "It's the product of an enema," I shouted over the din but they would not heed me, heaping up the turds of metal. I looked to my son and disciple, Peter, for comfort, but the fall was so thick that I could not see him. I struggled through the thickness to reach his bed, only to find him lifeless. The coins had fallen upon him with such weight that his breath was stopped. Coins filled his open mouth, spilled over in gilded vomit and settled all along his body so that he looked as serenely and splendidly dead as a Pharaoh. I gasped at the sight of one so arrayed in glory, so transfigured, and I turned to Stick for confirmation of the ordinary and the real. Stick was up to its neck in wealth, drowning in filth. I tugged at Stick's handle but it would not budge. I tried again, but failed. "Third time lucky," I whispered to myself, gripping the handle, and with mighty effort hauling Stick free. As I held it up like the fabled sword, a shaft of sunlight appeared from nowhere to emblazon us. The sight of Stick in an epiphany of light brought sudden stillness to the room then, after a long pause, a voice arose, and a second, a third, each gathering strength from the others. "A-R-F-U-R! A-R-F-U-R! A-R-F-U-R!" they chanted. I stopped my ears to their adulation, grabbing Stick and my bag of belongings. I trudged through the effluence, making for the door, but hands reached to pull me back and I groaned with the effort of climbing over the sovereign hills, cursing my hip as Moses would have cursed God for the existence of the sea. "May boils breed upon you, may desert sands blight you, may stars blanch as you approach and darkness blot out the sky," I cursed, seeking to outdo the First among Jews. It worked, for all were hushed. Then came the first voice of defiance. "She's the one, she's special, she's none other than Moses," it shouted. Stillness again, then the gradual rise of worshipful voices. "M-O-S-E-S! M-O-S-E-S! M-O-S-E-S!" they chorused, changing their tune. "Give us a miracle!" someone cried out. "Heal me, O wondrous one!" "A barrel of happiness, O blessed one!" "Never mind him, a spoonful will do me, just a spoonful, O crowned glory!" "A drop, a drop, a mere miserly mingy midge of a drop, O creature of bounty!" They hollered. They screeched. They wept.

"For Christ's sake, get us out of here," Stick commanded, resuming its old self. It turned on the throng, beating them back, whacking head and limbs cruelly. "Leave her alone, she's only Molly of Accrington," it shouted. "She's not Arthur, she's not Moses, she's a simple arse-over-tit common-and-garden matter-of-fact kind of person. In solemn truth, more slag than saviour, so shove off the lot of you. Avaunt and quit my sight!"

My instinct was to drop Stick, turn around, face them and pontificate like a proper prophet. I'd lower my voice an octave, give it a certain cadence, and begin to preach in riddles and parables. "A sower went out to sow, know what I mean?" "A skylark rose before the dawn, eh…?" "Three men set off in midwinter, get it…?" A wink here, a helpful clue given there, and the whole bloody lot would whoop in recognition then kneel down before me.

"Silly buggers," Stick muttered, condemning them to eternal helplessness. "Get a move on Molly," it urged but I stood my ground.

"I'll not go without Peter," I said, moving to his bed. "I'll save Peter, the two of us will live in my mother's dream. In my mother's mansion are many rooms, ancient and oak-beamed and set in land fertile and green and far away." I gazed upon Peter and sang to him, wanting to awaken him. "There-is-a-green-hill-far-away–" He bolted upright, my mouth stopped in fright as the coins were flung from his body. The lunatics scrambled as before to gather them up. "Get thee yonder to Coventry," Peter chided me, in Harold's voice. The realisation that Harold had possessed him suddenly wearied me. My urge was to tend to Peter, to bring him into original speech, as a mother nurtures a burble of her infant, encouraging it to intelligible sound. Harold, though, had denied me. He had soiled Peter's tongue. I was stupid to dream that I could regain motherhood after the doings of the pals. There would be no new life for me, no newness in my life. I surrendered to Harold. I abandoned Peter, I left him to the truth of the dead. The sole truth was death and to dream was only to give voice to the dead.

PART 3

Coventry – my future – was only so much of the past, so much death. Not the slightest redolence of Arthurian romance in the rows of terraced houses, nor did the canals evoke the Red Sea. The memory of death was everywhere, in the burnt shells of buildings and in craters where homes once were. The ugliness of the place must have affected Stick for as soon as we entered Coventry it fell silent. It was loquacious on the train, boasting to the other passengers about its fabulous status, telling them in a voice that rose above the rumble of the locomotive wheels that it was from Camelot; that it was a spirit of majesty but sadly imprisoned in wood by me, Molly the sorceress; that one day it would be freed from slavery and once more… I endured its spite and the hostile looks from the passengers, for I was secure in my future. I would find Harold's bank and open up an account there with the money he had given me. Harold was right: a bank was the logic of myself. No unruly shower of coins and sperm. Everything was counted, bagged and tagged in a bank. You put in ten pounds and that's more or less what you got when you returned to demand them back. No voices arising in your head, tempting you to believe that you were worth millions and deserving of a mansion and climax. A bank cured you more effectively than an asylum. Mad folk should be housed in a bank's vault and be subject to the truth of tellers, not the hocus-pocus and the pills of psychiatrists, their promise that eventually you'll pull through. Ten pounds would never "pull through" to a million; in a bank a deposit of a stick was a deposit of a stick was a deposit of a stick... The rhythm of the locomotive wheels comforted me, I stopped listening to Stick's bragging.

The train pulled into the station and Stick was dumbfounded. It was not the ugliness of Coventry that stilled it but the prospect of the bank. I took satisfaction in leaning on it more heavily than usual as we made our way through Coventry's streets. If it groaned under my weight it did so silently. I had reclaimed it to my will. Harold had prepared for my entry into Coventry. There was no guiding star in the evening sky but even in the darkness I located the bank. Harold had ensured that I would not be homeless, the building next to the bank was a boarding house, and rooms were available. I unpacked my bag, put away my belongings in various drawers – blouses in one, dresses in another, undergarments in a third – a sense of order returning to me. I placed Stick against the window which looked out to a school across the road. One day I'd teach there, I knew it, for Harold had planned my future. For now I'd wash the dirt from myself – the bath, though neither huge nor enamelled, was spotlessly clean. I'd lie between the fresh sheets and sigh myself to sleep, thinking of Terence. Let me be a teenager, hurt by romance and inconsolable. Let the weeks pass and the months. Let me nurse grief within me so as to strangle it at birth. Then freed of... what? What would the strangulation free me of? I didn't know. I was too weary to bother knowing. Let me sleep, let the night pass so that I could arise to a sun so melancholy I would doubt my awakening.

*

A year on, and all the arrangements to put my affairs in order had been made. I rented a house in an affordable area of Coventry and gradually redecorated it in simple – even bland – colours. I was appointed as a trainee teacher, the modest salary adequate for my upkeep. Modesty, affordability, adequacy – these were the qualities I resigned my life to. A statuette of the Virgin Mary gazed down upon me from the mantelpiece, approving of the chasteness of my new life.

My only acquiescence to the past was the purchase of a cat but even then I resolved to deny the possibility of trauma – savaged birds and garden mice – by belling it, and by not giving it a name. "What's your cat called?" Eileen asked on her first visit, Eileen, a History teacher in my school. She stretched out her hand to stroke the cat but it snarled at her and walked away with imperious gait. "Such a picture of the past, such arrogance," Eileen said admiringly. "What did you say her name was?"

"Oh I call her Leah," I said, surprised at the spontaneity of my lie. "She's originally from Leeds," I elaborated. "Her owner was a cloth manufacturer who fell on hard times. She was given away, somehow ending up in Coventry in a house for abandoned cats. The people who ran the house told me this."

"Lucky cat, to have ended up with you, Molly. What made you choose her over the rest of the cats?"

"Can't think, really. Except I took one look at her and there was a moment of mutual recognition." Eileen and I laughed. I decided I could trust her. It had been a long time since I'd laughed with another human being.

On her next visit Eileen brought an inscription which had been found in the Royal Tombs at cat-worshipping Thebes. She had typed out the inscription and made me tack it on the wall above Cat's sleeping basket. "Thou art the Great Cat, the Avenger of the Gods, the Judge of Words, the Pharoah of the Holy Circle." "How curious," I said, suppressing my dismay at the sudden introduction of paganism into my simple household.

"Not really. The Egyptians believed the cat represented the life-giving heat of the sun, it was the source of life itself," Eileen said. I didn't want the sun in my house and began to distrust Cat, interpreting her every action – the licking of her paws, the sharpening of her claws against the bark of a garden tree – as a sign of impiety. I should have torn up the inscription but I let it remain in case Eileen thought me ungrateful. Cat too changed her behaviour. Previously a largely silent creature she now began to meow regularly, each cry sounding different in pitch and tone and duration. She developed a bewildering array of voices. It was as if the inscription had inspired her to expression. "Don't be daft," I told myself, reassuring myself that there was nothing Egyptian about Cat, that there was no cause to fear a sudden outbreak of primitive violence. As to her new volubility, well, animals were odd, that was all. Just as children came into articulacy, so cats perhaps. Still, when she brushed against me I would resist tenderness. "I am not your Mummy," I told her, pushing her from me, but gently, for I still feared her potential for retaliation. And, as an added precaution, I removed the Virgin Mary to the top shelf of the bookcase, beyond Cat's reach.

*

When the doorbell rang I was preparing for the next day's lesson. Fourteen-year old youth forced to study *The Merchant of Venice* – an uphill task, a wearisome journey through an alien world of imagery and language. I planned to start with the geography of Venice. "Does anyone know where Venice is?" I would ask, fully expecting glum faces. Perhaps I would strike it lucky. Perhaps one boy collected stamps and would break the silence. Common sense told me that the furthest their parents could travel on savings from their social welfare cheques or black-market dealings were places like Blackpool or Skegness. Overseas places were out of their reach so I would settle for Coventry, and try to make some kind of comparison between Coventry's canals and those of Venice. Worlds apart, in truth, but I would still attempt some fusion.

The children stared at me with blank faces. White stupid faces. The blankness and stupidity all the more evident because of their whiteness. A doughy whiteness, absorbing but not reflecting light. Not for them the dread and the excitement of encountering the foreign. I looked out of the classroom to the row of pre-fabricated houses with their peeling paint-work, huddled together under a low sky, and was oddly comforted by their lack of imagination. I gave up on them, settling for the imparting of information rather than knowledge. My teaching was dutiful, dependable, the school was pleased with my efforts. I was content with the sequence of schooldays which passed without undue emotion, undue drama.

Cat was sitting at my desk staring curiously at me as I prepared the lesson on *The Merchant of Venice*, when the doorbell rang. Cat bolted upright, dug her claws in my sheaf of notes, then jumped off the desk, scattering my papers in the process. She ran into the kitchen and through the flap into the garden. I stooped to retrieve the papers from the floor but my hip suddenly locked into place. I tried to straighten my body but couldn't. I heard myself calling out to Stick. Twelve months had passed since we drew into Coventry station and Stick lost the faculty of speech. "Get real, get a grip on things," I chided myself for resorting to Stick's help. For all my coaxing my hip remained set in contempt of me. With mighty effort I rose from my chair and made my way to the door, my body curved in distress.

The presence at my doorstep gave off such a smell that I stepped back instinctively. Imagine a pigsty suddenly brightened by butterflies blown in by accident. Frantically they seek exit, the panic of wings begetting a strange perfume. Imagine the aroma of beating wings mingling with the vapour of swill and dung; an alchemy that makes even the morose swine raise their snouts from the trough and sniff the air delicately.

"Come in," I told the stranger, surprised by my hospitality, for I had grown to relish the solitariness of my house, Eileen its only visitor. Man or boy I couldn't be sure for the doorway was dark and I was looking at him from an odd perspective, my head pressed to my shoulder, the whole of my body an unsightly curve. I led him into the lounge and turned around to face him, shyly, overcome by a sense of my posture and my unloveliness.

"Do excuse the mess," I said, gesturing to the papers scattering to the floor by the cat's flight. I tried to utter some other banality by way of a greeting but my Accrington breeding revived my tongue.

"God's truth, you're a right black one aren't you?"

His clothes were flimsy, pasted to his body so that he appeared naked, his crotch bulging against thin cotton trousers. He shivered, sneezed, and a sycamore leaf fell from his hair. I gazed at the traces of bark and twigs caught there, and struggled for words.

"Sit you down, I'll make you a hot mug of tea," I said eventually, fleeing to the kitchen.

Stick was there to confront me. It had found its tongue. Hopping mad it was.

"Silly woman, how could you let a stranger into our house, and a nigger at that?"

It stopped jumping up and down, petrified by the word it had uttered. I too was affected by its fright.

"What should I do?" I asked Stick.

"You offered him tea, so go to it. Stir in his sugar, make small talk, we can at least show him our English manners, but as soon as he's done boot him out before he gets hungry and eats us."

I returned to the lounge with a tray of tea, bearing it as a tribute and offering to appease the savage's appetite. He was sitting on the sofa, staring at the opposite wall like a deity in repose. Stick followed me into the room and stood protectively beside me.

"Not a nice night to be out, the weather's foul, have you come far?" I said, placing a mug before him. "It's the way our weather is. One moment sunshine, the next hailstones and downpour. You're soaking wet, it must have caught you out. Best always to carry an umbrella in our country."

The savage continued staring into space, careless of my advice.

"One sugar or two? Milk?" I asked, but he remained silent. I poured tea with a steady hand and put on a cosy smile.

"My name's Molly, what's yours?"

Not the slightest flicker of reaction.

"Come on lad, don't be such a dead sardine," I said in an endearing voice, but he still would not connect. My Accrington mood reawakened.

"What's the matter? Cat's got your tongue? Who do you think you are turning up at my door at this hour, flashing your testicles? I've seen enough of those, I don't mind telling you, I don't shock easily."

"He's dismal, he's the devil's pup," Stick said, goading me to greater hostility. "Let me thwack him back to his benighted habitation."

"Let him be," I snapped at Stick, for the stranger had now turned to face me and I was once more awed at the revelation of flesh so burnished. "You're a right conker, you," I said, wishing I could conjure up richer words to describe his sheen. Sable. Opulent. Amber of the ancient East. A beauty extreme beyond the opalescence of our clime. It was my turn to pale into silence and his to speak.

"Wahwath kulla ara lish shana khadh mamla khadh," he said.

"My God!" Stick exclaimed, ignoring me when I turned to it for elucidation. It fell into deep contemplation, repeating the words the stranger had uttered. "Remarkable! Quite remarkable!" Stick muttered to itself.

"What's going on? Come to your senses, tell me what he said," I demanded.

"I do believe it's a mixture of Sanskrit and a Greek dialect, but all in pidgin," Stick said.

The stranger spoke again: "Zil bashlama waq ree shlame lawahayk."

Once more Stick ruminated on the words, then with great effort and concentration spoke some of the foreign gibberish. The stranger brightened, his tongue loosened, gushing out more gibberish to which Stick responded with alacrity. The two of them engaged in halting conversation, Stick pausing now and again to exclaim "Extraordinary!", "Quite amazing!", "What a language! More like Aramaic than anything else."

"Oh damn the lot of you!" I said, but before more curses against men could ferment in my mouth Stick hushed me with a lyrical utterance.

"He said you're not crooked but that your body is a crescent moon, that he is a moth drawn to an arc of white moon."

"He really said that, he did, did he?" I stammered, blushing like a young woman at her first experience of flattery. My hip unlocked all of a sudden. "What else? What's his name? How old? Where is he from? How's he got here?"

"Calm down, it'll take me a little while fully to figure out the language. He comes from a place where people don't have names or reckon their ages. Demerara, in the jungles of British Guiana. I'm not sure how he travelled here. If I understand him properly he *flew* in. In Demerara people apparently are not merely human but also partly winged or four-footed or crawling. All the creatures of the jungle are of one body, none of them are male or female, but neither and both. It's probably all bullshit. By the looks of him he's stowed away in the hull of a ship bringing a load of timber and bananas to this country."

I gazed upon the stranger again, trying to imagine him as a man-boy or boy-woman, ageless, sexless, an inhabitant of earth and river and air. "Poor thing! He's obviously loopy. You're right,

Stick, there's bits of vegetation pasted to his skin. He must have come over on a banana boat. And he smells like fruit force-ripened in darkness."

"Run him a bath before he stinks the place out," Stick suggested.

I bathed him myself, cleansing him of foliage, and he was passive in my hands. His nakedness was a novelty to me, for I felt no inkling of base emotion. Sometimes, the pals would insist on washing me before they left the house. Dad's enamel bath became a kind of baptismal font, they lowered me into it and cleansed the stains they had made on my body but I knew it to be a forced act of contrition, knew that Christ lowered from the Cross could not be restored to innocence, that no amount of winding sheet soaked in frankincense could mask His hurt. Still, I surrendered to the pals' deceit, or rather self-deception, for I wanted to believe that the devotion of their hands as they bathed me was their genuine pilgrimage into an understanding of the sickness they had made of their lives, and of mine.

I cleansed the boy-man, but with no emotion, neither lust nor in a mood of reparation. I was merely mothering him, for he was in a foreign land in the midst of strangers. I must have spent a suspicious length of time with him, for Stick entered the bathroom with accusation on its lips.

"What kept you? Even the engendering of toads takes less effort and time."

I hushed Stick, reminding it of our obligations to strangers. "You may have Moorish sap in you but you're of more recent stock," I scolded it. "You're not banyan or mangrove root, so cease your unruliness, remember your manners, in my house at least!"

Stick sulked as it watched me preparing the foreigner, a perfect image of green-eyed jealousy.

"Speak to him. Explain that he'll have to make do with one of my dresses, that we have no men's clothing in the house."

"A woman's dress? A dress?" Stick spluttered, offended on behalf of the foreigner. Its voice darkened, dropped an octave, taking on a threatening male tone as it remonstrated with me. I refused to surrender to its strategy. It was trying to claim male kinship with the foreigner, to free him from my possession, and it was my turn to be jealous. Or at least I pretended to be, for in truth I was anxious to form a bond between the two of them, partly because they shared a language, but mostly because I longed for family. Stick, my peculiar husband; me, needing the chastity of our wedding; and now the boy-man whom I would adopt as mystery and legendary child. Stick intuited my need. It softened, it began to offer advice and wax romantic.

"Not the polka-dot one, he'll look silly in it. Give him the plain red dress, it hangs sweetly on you, heightens your paleness in a way that pleases me and will bring out his blackness well. But we must acknowledge his sex, so gird him with your father's belt, and your father's pipe in his mouth will make him the picture of an Englishman, in spite of the woman's apparel."

Eileen came that afternoon. On entering the drawing-room she was confronted by the foreigner sitting on my sofa, freshly powdered, pipe in mouth, wearing a buckled dress. Being impeccably English, she took her place beside him, accepting my offer of tea and biscuits with only the slightest sign of anxiety.

"It's alright, you can talk, he won't take offence, he doesn't understand a word of English."

Eileen lent in my direction and whispered, "For God's sake Molly, who is he? What's going on?"

"I don't rightly know. I found him at the door, half naked and shivering. Poor thing, I had to take him in."

"Molly, you're a lone woman, you just can't–"

"Oh, not to worry, I have my stick to protect me. If he comes at me I'll just clobber him one."

Eileen frowned at my laughter, thinking me frivolous, but I would not surrender my mood. The boy-man's presence made me light-headed, it had been a lifetime since I felt so carefree. "As soon as he entered the house, I knew I was on the brink of some folly, but so what? Coventry's closing in on me, I'm beginning to feel cramped. How have you managed to survive here all these years?" Eileen refused to answer, not wanting me to deflect attention away from the boy-man. There was no need for her to answer for I already knew the limitation of spirit which made her suited to the place. Born in Coventry to a family of factory workers, her father a car mechanic, her mother an accounts clerk. A happy enough childhood, sailing toy boats along the canal with her brother, Sunday picnics, fruit picking for pocket-money. Nothing peculiar, nothing particularly memorable. Church schools, then teacher-training college; along the way the usual groping by men which left her unimpressed, unfulfilled. The war was the greatest excitement of her life, the explosions, the fires, the ashen skies, but the German bombing didn't last, she settled down to her studies and her teaching career. Her brother fell foul of the law for some minor misdemeanour and panicked, emigrated overseas, never keeping in contact. Now in her early forties and unmarried, she lived at home, caring for her elderly parents. She kept her mind active by devotion to her school duties, being Head of History. Her only distraction seemed to be an interest with things Egyptian, pyramids, hieroglyphs, divine cats and the like. It seemed like a mild fascination, not an obsession, for she never expressed a desire to visit Egypt. The furthest she went in pursuit of her interest was to the British Museum in London. I liked Eileen, she was harmless enough, and sometimes I envied the way she disciplined her life, whether consciously or not. Yet in her company I felt soiled, and after her Sunday afternoon visits I was compelled to run a bath. I used to think it was to wash away memory of my past, but I came to realise that I needed to purge myself of her smugness, her small, at times sanctimonious way of being. Yes, my past was unspeakable. But the extravagance of it at least gave me a desire for adventure. Eileen would have turned up her nose and calmly shut out the boy-man, whereas I let him in though I wanted to faint at the smell.

"Do you know, he's ever so confusing. To begin with he smelled of a swarm of butterflies, but that soon changed to rotting wood, then over-ripe fruit. I suppose it depends on his moods…"

Eileen looked stupidly at me, but I ignored her, awed by my speculation.

"Isn't that something? His scent depends on his moods! Is that what makes people like him different from us? Not their foreign language, or whatever food they eat, or how they dress… Those are all to do with culture, whereas he is different in *essence*, he is another kind of person altogether, another species. Do you think?"

"Oh leave off Molly, what's the matter with you? He's an ordinary boy, only black." Eileen put down her cup firmly, signalling her intention to go if I didn't come to my senses. I relented, not wanting to imperil our friendship. I needed her companionship, her presence reminding me of all the reasonable things I had been robbed of, whilst not fully regretting the deprivation. I looked at the boy-man dressed in woman's clothing and saw a partial image of my father, caught between innocence and stinking appetite, a butterfly in a pig-sty. I wanted to go up to the boy-man, to sniff at him, to acknowledge the cleanliness of his flesh, which yet smelt of the leather of my father's belt and the orifices of his tobacco-pipe, but Eileen's eyes were fixed on me, restraining me to my chair and ordinary chatter. We talked about the next day's lesson on Shakespeare, Eileen out of her superior experience volunteering tips as to how best to conduct the class and keep their attention.

*

Whatever little excitement or sense of achievement I felt as a teacher disappeared. Stick and I could hardly wait for the end of the school day, hurrying home to greet the boy-man, to tend to his needs. We stopped at the charity shop and bought him clothes suitable for his sex and the autumn weather. He was waiting patiently for us on the sofa. His face lit up when he saw Stick and the two of them entered into conversation whilst I tidied up the house and prepared tea.

"Does he mind if we have sausages and potatoes like last night, or something different?" I asked, but Stick was too immersed in trying out the new language to bother with such a common matter. I interrupted Stick, took the boy-man by the hand and led him upstairs to his bedroom. "Raise your hands," I said, imitating the action. He obeyed and I unbuckled the belt and lifted off the dress. I put him in a shirt, then signalling him to lift one leg at a time, I put on his trousers. He sat on the bed as I knelt before him, fitting his socks and shoes. Stick was at the doorway fretting. "Don't be a fool," I told Stick. "A child's nakedness is nothing to a parent." Stick, who had learnt the circumstances of my past – perhaps from my involuntary ramblings while in hospital – looked unconvinced. I changed tactic, assuming vulnerability and beseeching its help. "Please Stick, I need you to make him feel at home. He's probably accustomed to lying on the ground, show him how to change into night clothes and sleep between sheet and blanket. Teach him the use of the bath. And when I'm at school he must learn to make lunch for himself."

Such simple things, but they constituted our English identity, and Stick took its role as cultural tutor seriously. Before long, the boy-man was accustomed to our ways and even made tea when Eileen visited the following Sunday. He arranged the biscuits, pot, cups, spoons neatly on the tray and waited for the right moment before pouring out the brew.

"My, what a nice cup of tea," Eileen said, nodding appreciatively in his direction. I wasn't sure whether she was still scared of his foreign presence, the compliment being an attempt at pre-empting any sudden baring of teeth by him. "How's his English?" Eileen whispered conspiratorially to me when he went into the kitchen to fetch more sugar.

"Practically none, we're safe to talk."

"Have you not taught him anything? He's been cloistered here for a week, he must have picked up a little."

"Not really. He knows "bed", and "bath", and "teapot", a few words to get him by in the house. Next week's half term, I'll take him out then and show him the rest of England. It won't take long, there's not much around here – shop, bus stop, pub, butcher's – he'll quickly learn."

"So what does he get up to all day? He must be bored."

"Yes, bored, poor thing." I lied. Why tell her that when we tried to take the boy-man outdoors to walk in the park, he pleaded with Stick not to go? Poor thing, he came from faraway, the journey had wearied him, he merely wanted to rest in one place among pleasant and welcoming folk. And why divulge to her the happiness the boy-man had brought into my life by staying in my home? She would only think me crazy and shun my company or try by some subterfuge to end my happiness. My mind hesitated at the word "happiness" for I believed since childhood that whatever the word meant would never be my lot. But elation was what overcame me when I reached home to greet the boy-man, and a certain expectancy which made me blush like a shy teenager. I would be in the kitchen washing dishes, preparing our evening meal but not concentrating. My hand would slip, a saucer would break, but I didn't care, straining my ears to catch the conversation.

In the sitting room Stick and the boy-man were forever engaged in talk, sometimes gentle, sometimes furious. Stick delighted at its gradual acquisition of the language and the boy-man broke into laughter when Stick apparently misused a phrase. My home became a place of laughter. Even Cat overcame her fear, sat at the boy-man's feet, pricking her ears at this or that word, at times purring at him as if to signal consent. Only I was estranged from the chatter, but without resentment. I was content to look upon the three of them in peculiar harmony, and proud to be the one who made provision for them, cooking, sweeping, paying the household bills. I was integral to their lives, though bereft of words.

"What's the two of you yapping on about?" I would ask Stick, wanting to discover more of the boy-man's background, but Stick mostly ignored me. It guarded its monopoly over the boy-man, asserting its power over me by keeping me in a state of ignorance. Occasionally it would take pity on me and offer glimpses into an exotic and perilous world.

"Demerara, where he's from, is all jungle. That's why he smells of wood," Stick said proudly. "He's my human relation though the Demerara jungle is a different species of trees from ours. His is greenheart and mahogany and mora and helisong. They're not yew."

"No, they're not me, thank goodness," I said, but Stick dismissed my lightheartedness, refusing to speak further. "Go on, tell me more," I begged it, stroking its neck, promising to rub linseed oil along its length.

"Think of jaguars leaping from their lair of rock, think thunderous waterfalls, think creeks festooned with mangrove and crocodiles sliding between their roots," it said.

"And? And? What else?"

"Oh leave off, you tiresome woman! I'm still deciphering his tongue. What he tells me I'm not sure of, he's still an oddity to me. Perhaps I've got it all wrong, especially when he talks of winged humans, or communities of the dead at the bottom of the river carrying on like normal – making pots, mending their huts, hollering at their children – as if life on land and death under water are one and the same state." Stick paused to dwell on the curiosities the boy-man had divulged to it. "The more I discourse with him, the more I feel Muslim," Stick said at last in a voice trembling between horror and pride. Then it launched into a monologue, confessing to me that the boy-man made it feel unbearably old, half a millennium and more in age; how a fresh seed gathered up from Muslim lands by the hand of a crusader was sown in England, sprouted, flowered, and somehow mated with a native plant which in turn mated with another native plant, and another, so that the memory of Islam in the original seed faded with age, dunes echoing with the chants of the muezzin giving way to English forests and the song of nightingales. The final tree of which Stick was part was nourished in English soil for centuries. It was as ancient as cathedral, castle, or university spire. But now the boy-man reminded Stick of its origination. Oh, there was horror in the memory of Moorish slaughter, in the memory of the lascivious harem and slave market stinking with the sweat of terrified captives. But there was pride too. "We invented zero, the foundation of mathematics," Stick said, addressing me with fierce contempt for my Christian heritage. "When you lot were eating grass we Muslims were mapping the night sky, our architects were embodying the rules of geometry in marbled domes."

"Oh how are the mighty fallen!" I retaliated. "Nowadays you're truly zero, naught, nil, null, a big black bottomless bastard of a hole. And you lot spend all your time chasing camels. Or you stagger from one infested water hole to the next, cursing the sun, picking lumps of sand from your nostrils. And until recently you belonged to Harold the Jew."

"You blasphemous daughter of a pig, you vile progeny and very symbol of barrenness," Stick cursed, trying to sound Koranic. It raised itself as if to hit me. The boy-man spoke. I didn't understand a word, but he gave off a scent – sour, like mouldy cheese – that signalled alarm. Stick backed off and turned to him. Once more the animated gabble beyond my comprehension, except the word "zero" which cropped up frequently.

∗

"I know it's not part of his culture but let's name him anyway, seeing he's in England." Stick huffed at my suggestion then changed its mind, no doubt calculating that by coming up with a name it would cement its bond with the boy-man. I let Stick try out a few, turning each down with utmost politeness so as not to offend it.

"I know, let's call him Adam since he's from the New World and the first male to come our way," Stick said brightly.

After a show of cogitation I refused. "He's not the first bloke to come my way, but he'll be the last. Give him a name that signifies the end, beginning with 'Z' perhaps," I said, adding, "so long as it's not 'Zero'."

Stick thought hard, but nothing came.

"Zachariah? Zebidee?" I offered.

"No, too Semitic," Stick growled.

We decided eventually on Om, Stick shortening "omega" to give the word an ethnic edge, claiming that it sounded Hindu but also evoked the Muslim name Omar whilst retaining its roots in a Greek-Christian concept, and not a hint of Hebrew. The truth was the name started with a domineering "O" – the poor "m" looked little and redundant beside it – so Stick got its zero after all.

"Don't you think we should clear it with him?" I asked, but Stick was dismissive.

"Om is his name. He'll just have to answer to it," Stick said imperiously. "Let's do a ceremony, is there any beer in the house?"

I found a bottle and gave it to the boy-man. Stick addressed him in a sombre tone, then tapped him on the head and left and right shoulders, chanting the word "Om" at each gesture. Om nodded and drank the whole bottle in one prolonged gurgle. When he finished he wheezed, his eyes bulged. A minute later he lent to one side and attempted to vomit. He stood up as if to go somewhere, swayed, sat down again.

"Fetch another bottle," Stick commanded. "Let's tame the little savage properly, make him beholden to our beer, in thrall to our spirit."

I was shocked at Stick's cruelty, the recrudescence of his Muslim character. And a whiff of stale beer stayed with Om all during his stay in Coventry. No amount of soaking and powdering could get rid of it. Poor Om, we had given him a bad odour. We had besmirched his nature by our baptism ceremony. I blamed myself – everything that entered my presence eventually rotted. I was a living curse.

※

Which is why I tried to dissuade Carol from any relationship with me. I didn't want to spoil her, the brightest student in my class, the only one who responded with any fervour to *The Merchant of Venice*. She was from a council estate, so should have grown up to be servile and unimaginative. Carol, though, had a tartness to her, a fourteen year old with pert breasts and presence who could suddenly feign a girlish shyness which not so much endeared her to you as made her seductively unknowable. I could envisage her at eighteen or twenty-one making men more dangerous than they were, driven to despair or callousness over their futile attempts to fix her to the certainties of their desire. She would slip and slide between promising and spurning them. The promises would be so voluptuous that their withdrawal would cause unconscionable collapse. In the end men would want to stamp upon her, heel her into the ground, spade her under. "I will bring death in the shapes of men to you," I wanted to warn her, to keep her from a premature sexuality which would come because of association with me. Even so I encouraged her to seek contact with me, always addressing her first with my question about the text before seeking her classmates' views.

"I'm writing a story, Miss," she announced one day. I had remained in the classroom during the lunch hour to finish the marking of essays, not wanting to take them home, for the semi-literate scrawl and horrendous grammar would frustrate me, rob me of the delight of Om's company. I felt beholden to Om, especially after the error in giving him beer, and I would hurry home as soon as school ended to be with him. I resented the interruption, but there was such longing in Carol's eyes that I let her enter, put away the essays and prepared to listen to her.

"So what's your story, do you want to read it to me?"

"Not written it yet, Miss, it's still in my mind. Not sure I should tell really." She grew bashful, sprawled on the chair and wriggled her feet to make me notice her socks, cheap and elastic but brazenly red. School regulations specified white.

"It's about a suitcase," she blurted out, then twirled a strand of her hair coyly.

"A suitcase, what's in it?"

"A red suitcase and she's packing clothes into it one by one, folding them slowly and crying."

"Who's the girl packing clothes into the suitcase? Is it you?" I should have known the stupidity of my question. She was too bright for the ordinary conjecture about her state of mind: a fourteen year old contemplating running away from home, coming first to her teacher to confess.

"An old woman she is," Carol said, looking cunningly at me. "She's packing her man's things first, then some stuff for herself."

"They're off on holidays then, are they?"

The question seemed to amuse her, I sensed a hint of malice in her voice. "No, he's gone before. They took him away and she'll have to follow. That's why she's crying quietly to herself while she packs his things, Miss."

"Don't call me Miss, Molly will do." Instantly I regretted this, alarmed by the need for intimacy. She looked at me, wanting to discover the reason for my bewilderment. I shuffled my papers and arranged them into a neat pile as if to resume my marking but she twitched her feet again to show off her rude socks.

"I don't have a name for the woman but she's wearing a pretty dress."

"That's nice for her," I said, correcting an essay, head bent resolutely, pretending to ignore her.

"A green dress with a pattern of red flowers, that's what she's wearing, Miss," Carol persisted, innocent of what provoked my pen to veer off the page. It was Carol's turn to be alarmed.

"I can make her wear some other colour if you like, Miss – sorry, Molly."

"No, no, it's your story," I said and babbled on about a need for her to be true to whatever came into her mind. I was aghast at Carol's ability to glimpse into my past. I had thought that I would be the one to bring her death in the shapes of men, but it was she who was reminding me of my mother's accursed frock.

"Honest, Miss, the story's not yet finished, I can put the woman in pink or yellow."

I was suddenly moved by her vulnerability, her desire to please her teacher, her figure of authority. "Don't ever, ever, surrender to the likes of me," I said with such forcefulness that she looked away from me, gritting her teeth to restrain tearfulness.

"I didn't mean nothing, I only came to tell you how I hate Antonio, I hate Bassanio, the lot of them, only Shylock I feel for."

"They cheated Shylock, didn't they?"

"They sure did, and laughed, poor thing." Her eyes watered as if she would cry for Shylock, but I knew it was for me, that somehow she had unearthed aspects of my past.

"I'll tell you what, let's not bother with the Antonios in this world, let's just laugh that he ended up with that bitch Portia."

She took the bait and perked up. "Yes, that Portia's a right slag, dumb, ain't she?"

"If she had any sense she would have gone for the Prince of Morocco, never mind all that rubbish about caskets. Oh Carol, I bet you would have gone for the Prince of Morocco."

"Too right I would, his speech is lovely and strange."

"The Hyrcanian deserts and the vasty wilds of wide Arabia," I quoted and Carol giggled in excitement. "I'll let you into a secret. Can you keep a secret?" Carol nodded, becoming a child again. I leant towards her and whispered, "The Prince of Morocco lives in my house. Would you like to meet him?"

*

Each afternoon, Carol would come to the house, lying to her parents that she was cat-sitting for me. Like Cat she was initially fearful of Om. She sat opposite him sipping lemonade and scrutinising him.

"It's not nice to stare," I said.

She looked at me sarcastically. "I'm nice enough. It's him. He'll bring trouble."

"Trouble? What do you mean?"

"Trouble, that's all. It's written all over him, can't you see?"

I was too infatuated with Om to see and dismissed her warning. "He's harmless, poor thing, and far from home. Don't malign him."

"I think I'll put him into my story," she said.

"By all means, but don't make him scary. Make him handsome and mannerly and opulent, look beyond his blackness, which is more than that silly bitch Portia did."

"That's true. I never did take to the way Portia scorned Morocco's colour. What does 'opulent' mean?"

"I'll show you," I said, going to fetch a book on Christian art and finding Bosch's painting of the Adoration of the Magi. I explained the scene to her, dwelling on the figure of the black Magus. "Isn't he just something! Studded with pearls, and look at the embroidery of his coat, so rich, with strange animals from another world. Now that's what you call opulent, a figure worthy of worshipping the Virgin Mary. The other two Magi are plain and doddery beside him."

"Are you religious Miss?"

"Why do you ask?"

"You're so carried away when you talk, like you've got God on your mind." She pointed to the statuette of the Virgin Mary on the top shelf.

"I got that at a jumble sale. I'm not religious, not any more. When I was your age I used to read the Bible to my mother."

"Is Om a Christian like that opulent black man in that picture you just showed me?"

"I don't rightly know. He resembles that Magus a bit, doesn't he? The skin, the curly hair, the broad nose."

"And he smells of cathedral wood," Carol added. "I've been wondering what the smell was in the room, it's cathedral wood."

"How do you mean?" I asked, unnerved by her imagination.

"Haven't you been? There's a ton of planks in the shell of the cathedral that got bombed by the Germans. They're planning to build a new one and lorries are arriving all the time with wood.

Me and my mates passed by on Saturday to have a peek. The air is full of wood dust when they unload, like incense, but more raw. We sneezed, one after the other, then together, we were like a choir." She laughed at her own wit, throwing back her head, the ribbons on her plaited hair dancing on her shoulders. The sudden revelation of beauty hurt me. I wanted to hold her protectively to my breast, to whisper in her ears the green promise my mother once made me.

"You yourself resemble the Virgin Mary in the picture," I said. She smirked, stuck out her tongue and wriggled it, expressing disbelief. "No, have a look." I opened the book again to the nativity scene. "Her forehead's high and radiant, she's lovely with child."

"Oh Miss, stop it," she said, half pleased, half bemused, looking at Om and blushing. Om seemed to understand her confusion. He smiled as he gazed upon her and I was momentarily alarmed by his closeness to her.

Stick came to my rescue with pomp, punctilio and what it thought was appropriate language. "Desist from suppositions, chimeras and superfluity of conceits. I will assume suzerainty over the stranger and be bulwark against egregiousness, I will be our cassine, our circumvallation. I will don armour, cuirass, hauberk and wield such weaponry against any spirit that threatens coition, stupration, teratogenesis."

Poor Muslim! Stick must have suddenly felt alienated by our Christian company. Hence the procession and march-past of words which demanded salute and a fusillade of ovation. Foolish, selfish Stick, no wonder Om couldn't speak the simplest word of English, though a week or more in our house, I thought. And not wanting to break Stick's monopoly of the boy-man and provoke its ire, I had never attempted after our first encounter to address him.

*

The time for our outing came, Eileen having offered to take us to the British Museum on the first Saturday of the half-term break. The day before she had slipped on the pavement wet with autumn leaves. She had bruised her knee but still insisted on the trip. I dressed Om in a white shirt and a pale tie to highlight his burnished skin. Carol lingered outside the bedroom door but I wanted Om to myself. I let her sulk there. Om was my unexpected bounty, appearing at my doorstep one autumn night when my life was tethered to a stake, awaiting the assault of beastly memory. Perseus or the proverbial dark stranger or stuff from *Silas Marner*, silly, I know, but true all the same. Om was the promise my mother made me but never fulfilled, her death crippling me, tethering me to the stake that was my Stick. Om freed me into the prospect of an unknown future. The trip to London would be my first chance to flaunt my fortune, to display him to the outer world. I dressed him with selfish pride, keeping Carol at a distance.

As soon as we stepped outdoors it began to drizzle and I went back inside to find some protection for Om. There was nothing suitable except my father's cap. As I fitted it onto his head I was overcome with gloom. It was like degrading him, crowning him with thorns. Even Stick looked disapprovingly at the cap.

"Perhaps we should go another day," Carol suggested, prescient as ever to our coming trials.

"Oh brighten up you lot, it's only a light drizzle. Liquid sunshine. It will not spoil our trip one jot," Eileen chided.

The train was packed and the air suffocating, the windows closed because of the rain which poured down with malice. The five of us were huddled in silence, for speaking would only increase our discomfort. Words uttered would take up space, cramping the carriage even more. People glanced furtively at Om, and I was sure that if other seats were available they would have moved out of sight. He himself was a picture of discomfort, stuffed in an autumn overcoat, his eyes glowing from underneath the oversized cap which concealed the whole of his forehead. He stood out in our crowded company but when the train went through a tunnel he merged into the darkness and vanished altogether. The four-hour journey to London saw him appear and disappear, to the obvious delight of a boy who sat with his mother two seats away. Half way to our destination he broke loose from his mother and sidled up to Om.

"Peter!" I exclaimed when I set eyes on him, then stopped my mouth with my hand. I looked to Stick for conformation of the boy's identity, for he was the very image of Peter whom I used to nurse in my asylum days. Stick twitched in my hand, the edge of its handle dug into my palm, ordering silence.

"Are you Peter?" I asked the boy tenderly, letting go of Stick and reaching out to lift him onto my lap. Stick fell against Eileen's bruised knee, she gave out a little yelp of pain and frowned at me. I withdrew from the boy and retrieved Stick. Carol fidgeted in her seat, wanting to distance herself from the unfolding drama.

"Stephen, come back here at once," the mother barked, but the boy wouldn't listen, captivated by Om's presence. He tiptoed and stretched out his hand, wanting to touch Om's face. Om leant back but the boy insisted, attempting to climb upon Om's knees.

"Stephen!" his mother shrieked. Her cry must have unsettled Om for he gave off an unpleasant smell and spoke a word to the boy. The mother, at the edge of her patience, arose to retrieve her son. But the train lurched at that very moment, throwing her against her neighbour, an elderly man who spluttered as the mother's head thudded into him. He rubbed his chest and groaned piteously, then leant forward, vomiting over the knees of the passengers opposite before collapsing at their feet. Pandemonium! Cries of panic, disgust, and an outbreak of movement when all before was stiffly silent. The train suddenly entered a tunnel, throwing all into darkness, and when it emerged the boy was prostrate in the aisle, his hand still outstretched, but now pointing to the roof of the carriage and to the heavens beyond instead of at Om. I immediately rose and went to his aid shaking him, trying to lower his arm, but it was as if locked in rigor mortis. The mother, seeing me bent over her boy, let loose a scream which was swiftly drowned out by the train's hooting as it approached another tunnel.

One old man in a daze, one young boy unconscious, and we had not yet reached London.

"Serves him right," Stick muttered as the boy was stretchered off at the nearest station, his hand still raised in a strange salute. The carriage emptied, people hurrying out to join another. As they exited, passing Om, they looked away or lowered their eyes.

"Serves him right," Stick repeated in defence of Om. "He'll know better next time not to poke at strangers. But at least we've got the carriage to ourselves, we can stretch out, eh?"

Eileen sat in shock for the rest of the journey. I had suggested we disembark and curtail our trip but she was determined to go on in spite of her nerves. Bruised knee; dazed, unconscious or vomit-splattered passengers; none of these would stay her appetite for things Egyptian. Her monthly visits to the British Museum were her only voyages into the exotic, helping to make bearable a life spent in the drab environment of Coventry. As to Carol, she wore an air of seclusion, as if the chaos had been foreseen and was therefore of no novelty. Om's malodour was still strong but disguised by the stench of vomit so we were not discomforted by his presence. His inner distress was not visible on his forehead for it remained covered over by my father's cap. Only Stick was agitated, cursing the boy I called Peter whom I once craved as a son.

More was to come! The hieroglyphs room was an oasis of calm, the visitors surging instead towards the chamber of mummies. Stick moved from one stone inscription to the next, translating for Om, showing off its expertise. I followed it dutifully, now and again sighing as it launched into tedious detail about some Pharaoh or the other. Eileen took my sighs to be expressions of awe at the antiquities.

"Marvellous, aren't they?" she beamed.

I had never before seen her so bright in spirit. That the rubble of the past should so excite her increased my curiosity about her character. I found myself pitying her, and pitying my own future. Would I, when I reached her age, still be dwelling in loneliness? A spinster school-teacher, outwaiting my students until I arrived at a pensionable age and the indignities that old ladies endured? I stood beside Om as he studied the stone ruins, and in a room of pagan superstitions I made a wish that he would never abandon me.

"Let's join the queue for the mummies," Eileen said, taking me by the hand and leading me towards the death chambers. Carol hesitated and Om stood his ground.

"Hurry up the two of you," Eileen ordered but they paid no heed. "We've come all the way from Coventry, the mummies are the highlight of the exhibition," she urged.

"I don't want to see them," Carol sulked.

"It's alright Carol, if you're scared you can hold onto me," I offered, twining my arms in hers.

"I'm not scared, it's just…"

It was only when Stick said something to Om and Om made to follow us that Carol yielded. We filed past the corpses, gazing at them without knowing how to respond. Even Eileen was stilled by them. I thought the display under the bright chandeliers sacrilegious. They belonged to their stone tombs, lidded and buried deep, not unwrapped and exposed to our gawking. Om too seemed troubled by the spectacle and began to smell of wormwood. Carol ignored the bodies, fixed her gaze on the exit sign. She was desperate to leave. She pressed her hand against her belly.

"What's the matter Carol?" I whispered, sensing she was in pain. Before she could answer a scream pierced the silence of the room.

"Allahu Akbar!"

I looked back to see a man in Arab dress holding a dagger aloft.

"Allahu Akbar!" he screamed again, slashing at the crowd which broke in all directions. The momentum of bodies shoved us towards the exit, so that without Stick's resoluteness I would have tumbled to the floor. Uniformed attendants – burly, red-faced men – rushed past us, pushing people aside in their haste to arrest the Arab. We linked arms and forced our way back to the room of hieroglyphs. Eileen was breathless, her face glowing with excitement.

"It's alright, nothing to worry about," she gasped. "Ever since we teamed up with the French and the Jews to threaten Suez, Egyptians have been coming to the British Museum to reclaim what they accuse us of plundering from their pyramids. We are lucky to have witnessed it first hand. It'll be in all the papers tomorrow."

"Poor Arab," I said, more for Stick's benefit. I had not the least interest in world affairs, though it did intrigue me that some imperial war at the far side of the world should have direct impact on small folk like us. "Are you alright?" I asked Om, who smelt slightly rancid. I slid my hand into his reassuringly. "Poor Arab," I said again, this time with conviction, for I was speaking out for the likes of Om. Eileen was alarmed by my sentiment.

"Hush Molly, there'll be trouble if someone hears you! Times like these call for patriotism."

"Theft is theft, no lesser if you're British or bog Irish," I said stubbornly and in a raised voice so as to provoke a response. I would have continued to berate the keepers of the museum but Carol suddenly tugged my skirt.

"I need the toilet, Miss," she pleaded. Her face was pale with horror. "I need to go now, Miss," she said, tugging desperately at me.

A trickle of blood, fresh, bright, dangerous, beautiful. Her first menstruation, wholly unexpected, brought on perhaps by the calamities of the day. I gave her a handkerchief to stem the flow. I tried to explain what was happening to her but she stopped me briskly.

"I know Miss, my other friends have it," she said, partly in pain, partly in pride. Now that the bleeding had started the horror had given way to a sense of achievement. From now on, I thought, she would be even more difficult to deal with. She'll grow even more brazen. She'll try to take Om away from me. I looked again at her stained thighs, remembering my own so many bleak years ago, and I relented. I drew her to me, hugged her urgently.

*

Suez. The newspapers' lead story for weeks. The war only lasted for a few days but its aftermath – the escalation of Cold War rivalries in the region – held the nation's attention for months afterwards, so it seemed. At the outbreak of hostilities we said morning prayer in school for our own; the children were put to fundraising, rattling collection boxes outside shops or weeding gardens for a donation to our valiant, embattled soldiers. The headmaster set them a project, an exhibition on the darkest moments of the empire – Iswandhala, the Black Hole of Calcutta – when British folk, beleaguered and outnumbered, still managed to survive and triumph morally over the barbarians. The children painted, discovering hidden resources of the imagination, and the images were displayed in the Town Hall, headlined in the local newspaper, the mayor opening the exhibition with a stirring call to arms. Each afternoon Carol and I escaped the rising hysteria by coming home to our own alien, Om. The newspapers, warning of secret agents and traitors in our midst, coined the phrase "the Red under the Bed", but Om was our nigger in the woodpile. He was our secret and we hid him from sight, guarding him from the ignorant hostile world outside my door. Om was happier than ever to stay indoors. The visit to the British Museum had not been to his liking. All day he sat on the sofa smelling of cedar or some other seductive bark, Cat his only company. Cat perched on his shoulder or curled up at his feet, a picture of appeasement. Carol, at first uncertain in Om's presence, staring at him suspiciously, grew bolder at each visit. Now she rushed up to greet him, hopping onto the sofa, taking his hand in hers.

"You don't think any more that he's dangerous? You warned me, remember?"

"Of course he is Miss, just look at him."

"He looks alright to me, serene in fact."

"What's 'serene', Miss?"

"Content, peaceful, happy."

"That's what you think. He's a beast underneath."

"Oh Carol, stop it! I thought you were brighter than all that beauty-and-the-beast stuff."

"Alright then, he's not a beast but he's sore underneath, reddish, raw. If you scratch he'll growl, and go to bite, like Cat when she doesn't want to be touched."

Cat, hearing her name called, pricked her ears and looked at Om for flattery. I laughed at the three of us, Carol, Cat and me, vying for Om's attention.

"I put Om in my story but then I took him out."

"Oh yes, your story, you've not mentioned it for a long time. How far have you got with it?"

"Not far, apart from putting Om in it." She squeezed his hand affectionately and shifted closer to him. Om gushed, the room was suddenly refreshed with a new fragrance. Carol giggled and blushed. I envied her schoolgirl's bashfulness.

"I'll make us a snack," I said, spurning her coquetry by going to the kitchen.

"Don't you wish he could talk to us?" Carol asked, taking up a slice of orange and offering it to Om's mouth. Om sucked upon it noisily; I was disappointed by the loss of serenity, the hint of coarseness which Carol appeared to inspire.

"I prefer him the way he is, quiet," I said, suppressing my jealousy. "There's too much talk in the world, talk, talk, that's all we do. Our mouths are like guns going off in other people's faces. I'd rather have the melody of animals, a soft purring, a birdsong."

"That's nice Miss, that really is," Carol said, her sincerity disarming me. "I wish I had the words that you do and could put them down in a nice way."

"But you are good with words," I encouraged her. "You should continue to write your story."

"The truth is I'm stuck, I can't see to write. I've got the woman and her suitcase but I don't know where she's going and why, and what happened to her man. I don't know nothing." She paused, dwelling in self pity.

"Why don't you give them a baby?" I offered.

"A baby?" Carol looked quizzically at me.

"Yes, because then there's another person to deal with, the story can go on."

"Do I have to tell the sex and all that, how they made the baby?" Carol asked.

It was my turn to blush.

"I know all about the sex," she continued, but I put on a face of indifference. "Don't you want to know how I know?"

"A story can be general, you can suggest, you don't have to go into detail."

She brushed aside my attempt to be teacherly. "But that's the best bit, Miss, the sex, or else it's boring."

"It's not," I said sourly, wanting to end the conversation. She stared at me, seeking disclosure. I resented her ability to pry into my life, to foresee my past and her future.

"Well, give up the story, perhaps that's best," I said, handing her another piece of fruit. "Or, let it rest for a while, until you get some inspiration."

"That's why I started to put Om in it, but I wasn't sure, so I crossed him out. Perhaps I should put him in again."

"No, don't. He's not part of us, best to leave him alone." I was anxious that Om should not be given speech in her story in case he told her luscious things. "Your body an arc of crescent moon," I said.

"That's nice Miss, that's really nice."

"It is, isn't it? Do you think you could come up with words like that?"

"Me? No way. I wouldn't have a clue."

"Of course you can't. You're too young, so best to leave Om alone. Drop him from your thoughts. Let your story be about Coventry people. And let the woman be by herself – she's too old for a baby anyway."

*

Her afternoon visits which once gave me the pleasant illusion of family began to wear upon my nerves. She flopped down on the sofa beside Om and stretched out her legs, resting them in his lap. She wriggled her ankles to show off her red socks. When she raised her legs playfully in the air her skirt slipped down her thighs, exposing her undergarment, the same brazen colour as her socks.

"Carol, cover yourself," I shouted, the sternness in my voice taking her aback.

"What's the matter Miss, what have I done wrong?"

"Don't play the innocent with me. You know what I'm on about." Without waiting for a response I retreated to the kitchen to regain my composure. It was spotless, as was the rest of the house, Om having taken it upon himself to clean whilst I was away working in school. At first I was grateful for his efforts, the windows cleared of stains, the kitchen floor mopped, everything dusted down and replaced. But now I began to doubt his motive. Was he cleaning it out of gratitude to me, or was he preparing the house for Carol's visits? My anxiety increased when he began to speak to her. To be sure, only a word now and then, but it was their secret and it hurt me when she laughed at what he said, as if relishing his flirtation.

"Don't be daft," Stick told me, reading my thoughts. "He talks to the cat too, haven't you heard the two of them parleying?"

"What's he saying to her?" I grilled Stick, not caring to disguise my emotion.

"I don't know exactly, in his tongue it is probably the same as our 'duck' or 'dearie'. A term of endearment, nothing more."

"Are you sure?"

"Oh leave off Molly, you're being the silly woman you are!"

I could have traded insults but I was vulnerable, I needed Stick on my side. "Aren't you worried Carol's taking up all his time? Go on, admit," I said to Stick.

"She's only a young girl, peckish and flirtatious. What's there for me to worry about? He needs me for conversation. It's you who are redundant."

"I may not be as attractive to him as that tart, but it's my house. I can turf the lot of you out."

Stick brought me back from the brink of desperation. "Come on Molly, he loves you, that's why he's not moved on. He'd happily spend the rest of his life in your company."

"What about her?" I asked, refusing to give in easily to Stick's attempt at reconciliation.

"What about her? What's there to say? She's seen blood run down her thighs, so she thinks her time has come, but it's only adolescent ego and provocation. She doesn't intend anything."

"She's more mature than you think, Stick. Didn't you hear her the other day saying she knows all about sex?"

"Bravado, that's all. She's all pertness and talk, no action."

"I hope you're right, I hope she doesn't get herself into trouble with Om. He's such a helpless soul, sitting on the sofa and staring thickly into space. Has he really got a brain in his head, apart from knowledge of housecleaning? I think he's something of an idiot."

"He's a bit stunted, that's true, when it comes to understanding our ways, electricity, or the engineering needed to make a train. But he knows his own world. He knows trees."

"Trees?" I began to scoff at Om's paucity of knowledge but remembering Stick's origin I stopped.

"Yes, trees, on this earth and in the other worlds. He has acuity of vision, he can probe beneath the density of surfaces and picture the existence of the living dead."

"Oh you do talk such nonsense Stick! I've long come to the knowledge that the dead are truly dead. Everything else is fantasy and craving."

Stick was not listening, immersed as it was in the mystery of its utterance. When, at last, it spoke, it was to accuse me of narrow-mindedness. "Consider me. I've existed for centuries in different climes, across cultures, in different forms, and countless unfathomable accidents and pathways brought me finally to your hand. Doesn't that constitute a philosophy above and beyond your blinkered seeing and scaly eyes?"

I would have none of it. I would not be bullied by its complexity. "You only speak because I dream you into being, and when I choose to wake you will revert to inertia. You are my madness made voluble, but reason reveals the hard edges and silence of the coffin. Reason is the reality I have chosen to repress so as to bring you into being for my own amusement. And when I tire of you I will shut you up and shut you away in the silence of the coffin. So don't call me a silly woman again, and don't try to pull the wool over my eyes with all your clever talk, or you'll be done for."

"So you're not just an aged carcass, a philosopher resides within," Stick mocked, refusing to be cowed.

＊

My home was no longer mine. Carol appeared every afternoon and at weekends, no longer bothering to be invited. She draped herself over Om, exposing her flesh. Cat was happy in their company, jumping at Om's lap and demanding in multiple tones of purring to be stroked. Stick too abandoned me, vying with Carol for Om's attention. Stick said something to him, he threw back his head and laughed, his ringlets rippled on his shoulders, rich and beautiful and painful to behold.

"You look vexed," Eileen said, examining me deeply as if I was one of her Egyptian curiosities.

"Oh, I'm just tired, that's all. The cold is getting to my bones."

"They say it'll be the coldest winter in memory."

"Is that so? I'd better stock up with coal and tinned food."

Our talk, aimless at the best of times, dwindled into silence. She watched Carol frolicking with Om and the cat and I sensed the sadness affecting her.

"They're a bit boisterous. Even the cat is trying out new voices," I said, teasing her into new conversation.

"Oh I don't mind their noise one bit. My own house is like a morgue, I can hardly get a word out of Mum and Dad. It's as if they've folded into themselves, hibernating, waiting for the end."

I was startled by her directness. She had never before spoken so bleakly of her parents. "It must be hard to look after them. Mine are dead, I've been spared."

"It's not hard in terms of work. Both are bedridden, they wake up only to be fed, and I've got a maid who comes daily to change their nappies and clean them."

"Still, after a long day at school, putting up with screaming brats, you'd want to go home to a little peace."

"That's the worst part, going home to silence. I'd rather have the children swearing and slamming doors any day."

"Eileen! I've always thought of you as a disciplinarian."

"Not really. I've had discipline all my life, I suppose that's why I became a history teacher, out of habit of putting things in place, neatening them."

"I'm the opposite. My young life was a mess, and today, without Om, the house would be just the same."

We paused, both of us on the brink of intimacy, calculating whether to go on or to retreat.

"You've never told me much about your past, in fact next to nothing," she said, testing my willingness to engage with her.

"You neither," I said, waiting on her to initiate our deeper friendship. Fortunately Carol distracted us. Om must have said something to her because she squawked and rolled off the sofa.

"Don't you dare, you monster!" She looked up at him, challenging him to continue whatever it was he had started. And when he looked bewildered she burst into laughter. "Poor Om, poor little monster," she cooed, stroking his face.

When we resumed our conversation, it was not about my pals nor about the mishaps which doomed Eileen to spinsterhood and care for her elderly parents. Her life would remain forever distant, subject to muddleheaded or prescient speculation on my part. In truth I preferred it that way, not wanting to be bonded to her through mutual confession of our murky pasts.

"It'll be Christmas soon, my, how time flies," she said.

"I suppose I should start planning something of a party maybe, drinks and a little dinner. Will you come?"

"It depends on the state Mum and Dad are in. Hard to tell. Christmas is always an anxious time for me. Old folk tend to die then. All over the country, a harvest of old folk, the grim reaper busy sharpening his scythe."

"Don't be so depressing Eileen! It's the season of merriment."

"No, it's true. The cold gets to them, or loneliness if they've got no relatives, or worse, relatives who don't bother to call around with a present and a pie. To think that a pair of socks gift-wrapped and a piece of mutton are all that stands between them and the desire to die! Life's a funny business."

"I've got Om, thank God," I blurted out. I could feel my skin blushing. I coughed out of embarrassment and couldn't stop until Eileen leaned over and slapped me on the back.

"I don't know what's come over me," I said, tears running down my cheeks.

"Coal dust, that's all," Eileen said, kindly, pretending not to understand. She got up and turned the fire over. She stooped before the grate, staring into the flames to blind herself to her misery. Missed opportunities for love and marriage. Parents who, in her youth, probably policed her encounters with men, imprisoning her to their presence, especially after her brother had absconded. Parents who grew old and dependent, drinking up whatever sap remained in her. Spinster, schoolmistress, solitary being: she fed fresh coal into the fire, dwelling on her aging self. I looked at her and saw my own future, my endurance of the ghost and the memory of parents and pals long dead who still awakened me to their bodily needs.

"No, I will not, will not," I hissed, flailing my hands at Harold.

The room fell silent. I could hear nothing but the cackle of flames, until Carol spoke.

"Miss, are you alright?"

I glowered at her. My mouth opened to curse her in language so obscene that even I was repelled by my aggression. I heard the words pouring fourth and recognised them as the words the pals would utter involuntarily in the delirium of orgasm. Then all was silent again. The silence of spent passion, as familiar as the sob that then issued from Carol in the wake of my battering of her. "I'm sorry, I'm so sorry," I wanted to say to her in the voice of my father, and to ruffle her hair playfully, to caress her face, to tickle her neck, as he used to do afterwards, trying to restore me to a loving child.

*

I passed Eileen several times in the school corridor, but she made excuses not to speak and carried on, clutching books protectively to her chest. At the end of the day I found her in the staff room, unable to escape me, for there was no one else there to distract her.

"I'm sorry, I don't know what came over me. I hope I didn't alarm you. It's just that sometimes things become too much, voices boom in my head…"

"I know. It's alright. We all get to breaking point." She spoke curtly, like a schoolmistress to an errant child. I was grieved by her perfunctoriness. She sensed my unhappiness but would not relent. "There's nothing to worry about, nothing at all. Just go home and rest, you'll be better after a good night's sleep." She turned away, focusing on papers on the notice board as a way of signalling that I was dismissed.

Carol was waiting for me outside the school gate. I greeted her apologetically, going to hug her, but she turned away and sulked.

"It's your fault, Miss," she said.

"Oh Carol, will you not forgive me. Please Carol! I didn't mean to curse you, it wasn't my voice but someone else's."

"The cursing is nothing to me Miss, it's what you've done to her."

"I know I've upset Eileen, and I'll make up to her and to you."

"To me but not to her. You've sent her away. She's the old lady in my story, packing a suitcase to go and never come back." She deepened my confusion by adding, "You'll see, just wait and see."

There was nothing more I could say to her to restore our relationship. I went to touch her shoulder but she brushed aside my attempt at affection and walked away. Once more I looked to Stick for guidance and it responded out of abiding love and pity for me.

"Invoke the spirit of Om, speak his name loudly or you'll lose her forever."

"Om, what about Om?" I called after Carol, stopping her in her tracks.

"What about Om?" she asked, turning to face me defiantly.

"You promised him."

"Promised? What?"

"Tell her about preparations for Christmas," Stick whispered.

"You said you'd help decorate our house for Christmas. He'll miss you if you don't. You don't want to hurt poor Om, do you?"

Stick's tactic worked, for Carol hesitated, twirling her foot around a paving stone as if drawing pictures. Pictures of balloons and streamers pinned to the wall, a Christmas tree hung with bulbs.

"I'm going to the shops right now, and tomorrow and the rest of the week. Come with me for Om's sake."

Each afternoon we went shopping and by Saturday she seemed to have forgiven me. A normal child, I thought, unable to sustain a grudge, casting off hurt and renewing herself, not like the creature I had become. Her spontaneity with Om no longer goaded me to jealousy. It was a child's joy in a new plaything, that was all, I told myself.

"Let's put up the decorations now," she urged, rifling through the bags and pulling out a bundle of tinsel.

"It's only October, Carol, it'll bring bad luck if we don't wait until December."

"But that's only two months away, Miss," she protested, looking at Om for support. Om, not understanding the subject, nevertheless beamed at her and released an odour which I imagined to be frankincense.

"I'll tell you what, let's leave the tree and the decorations for the proper time, but you can start making the crib now." I brought her string, paper, glue and some rags, and she set about her task in high excitement.

*

In the first week of November 1956, a British patrol boat was sunk in the Suez Canal by an Egyptian fishing boat packed with explosives. Among the five people who died was a young sailor from Coventry. Although the news barely registered with the nation as a whole, memories of the way the city was bombed during the Second World War roused Coventrians to wrath. The local newspaper screamed revenge against the barbarians of the East. Collection tins were rattled on every street corner, raising money for the bereaved family. Churches, normally half-empty on Sundays, pealed their bells and provided extra seating for the crowds. Many took to draping their garden gates with the Union

Jack. Hundreds marched through the streets with banners, ending up at the Town Hall to sing hymns of defiance. The whole city, it seemed, was hysterical with the spirit of patriotism. Except Eileen.

"Poor Egyptian fishermen," she said. "Think of the despair and the righteousness that made them blow themselves up. Were they among the five who died, or did we not bother to count them?"

"What's come over you Eileen, only last month you hushed me for taking the Egyptian's side."

"I was wrong," she said bluntly, then retreated into sullenness. "I was protecting you, that's all."

"Protecting me? I don't need protecting. I've got my stick."

She laughed scornfully. "You're an odd sod, that's what you are. Odd sod with a rod, you need protecting against yourself."

Never before had she shown rudeness towards me; I was unsure of how to respond.

"Don't bother to show me out," she said, rising from the sofa. "I'll not be coming back."

"Eileen, what's come over you? Have I wronged you?"

"Best to stay away from me," she said, a hint of threat in her voice. Cat, as if summoned by her mood, ran up to her and brushed against her legs conspiratorially. Eileen opened her handbag, took out a leather collar, stooped and placed it around the cat's neck. "It's my Christmas present to her. There's a hieroglyph carved in it." Cat scratched at the collar and purred with pleasure.

"Stay, Eileen. Carol will be here in a minute. She's making Christmas decorations with Om, she'll be glad for your encouragement." Om was sitting on the floor, carving a piece of wood into a bird, newspaper spread around him to catch the peels. He was as innocent of Eileen's mood as he was of the newspaper headlines railing against foreign savages.

"It's because of him that I shan't be returning," she said mysteriously. She softened as she looked at him, then before she could betray a deeper affection, turned to the door and left the house.

*

"I told you Miss, didn't I? I said you'd drive her away."

"But Carol, I've given her no cause. She just upped and left in haste. In all the Sundays she visited she never revealed herself capable of rudeness or unpredictable behaviour."

"You must have said something nasty to her, are you sure you didn't Miss?"

"I'm certain. One minute we were talking about Egypt, the next she bolted from the house. She said she was going for Om's sake. Strange that, I never thought she took to Om."

"She didn't. She was always suspicious of him. Remember how she'd stare at him, never saying a word? The only kindness she ever showed him was the trip to the Museum."

"Oh well, perhaps she just had a funny turn. I dare say she'll be back next week. Anyway, how's the crib coming along?"

Om and Carol sprawled out on the floor, bending wire and gluing bits of paper. I wanted to join in but was fearful that if I stooped my hip would lock and I would make a fool of myself trying to stand upright again. I watched them from afar as they made preparations for the baby and once more felt a twinge of jealousy. They were excited, fumbling with wire and paper, laughing, like a couple at the onset of love, preparing for a deeper intimacy.

"Om's so clever, he's carved baby Jesus, so beautiful," Carol said, glowing with delight and looking to me to approve of her admiration of him. "What's the matter, Miss, you're upset?"

Quickly I shook off my pique and lied. "Oh, I was worrying about Eileen. Silly me, she'll be back, I'm sure."

Eileen was absent from school the following week. The headmaster was not particularly concerned, Eileen having taken time off in the past on account of her bedridden parents. I was racked by anxiety, however, fearing that something regrettable had befallen her. Sunday came, I waited indoors all day with a freshly baked cake to greet her, but she stayed away. Two more days of absence from school and such dread in my mind that I could barely bring myself to face the class. I reverted to the state of a novice teacher, breaking chalk against the blackboard, butter-fingered with the Shakespeare book. The children eyed me curiously or giggled when my back was turned. I began to lose control of the class, the children ignoring me and talking among themselves or throwing pencils at each other as darts. In the midst of growing chaos the Headmaster suddenly appeared. He was pale and I prepared myself instantly to be reproached.

"I'm sorry, I've not been well, the children have got out of hand," I stammered.

He looked obscurely at me and led me out of the class. "It's not you that concerns me but her," he hissed, shoving the day's newspaper to my face. "You're her closest friend among the teachers. Tell me what's going on."

I had to lean against the wall for support, the news of Eileen was so shocking. There was a photograph of her holding up a placard outside the munitions factory on the outskirts of Coventry. **MURDERER** it read, the word all the more powerful because of its singularity. The accompanying article had as its title: "Traitor to Coventry and to History".

"What's she doing to us? Why is she bringing shame to our school?" the Headmaster was demanding, but I couldn't answer for the words were a blur. I concentrated hard to get the story but he kept interrupting me. As had become usual in such a situation I reverted to crudity, even against my will.

"Just fuck off will you, you piece of pompous turd."

The Headmaster's jaw dropped. He stumbled backwards, away from me.

"What is going on in my school? What madness is taking hold?" he muttered, looking me up and down as one would a creature from another planet, or from Egypt.

A week's suspension was my fate, preliminary to a disciplinary hearing, but I was more concerned for Eileen. I could feign a nervous breakdown and the onset of madness before the disciplinary committee, gain their sympathy and sickness leave. Eileen was bound to be dismissed, or worse. Once more I sought the counsel and support of my rod.

"She's a brave soul, she stirs the memory of Islam in me, works me up to a rage," Stick said.

"She's probably deserving of whatever medals you Muslims hand out to martyrs, but at the end of the day she's a mere Englishwoman, not a bloody Moor. Let's visit her, talk her out of disaster."

The next afternoon Stick, Carol and I set off for the munitions factory. Cat was eager to join our expedition, following us to the bus stop. I shooed her away but she stood her ground. Only when I raised Stick over her did she retreat down the road towards our house, pausing to look back resentfully. The bus dropped us off outside Eileen's encampment. She had set up a makeshift tent across the road from the factory gates, a piece of tarpaulin stretched over poles stuck in the earth. She sat inside, on a wooden crate, warming her hands over a weak fire, coal lit in a large saucepan but yielding little heat because of the damp. A rolled-up sleeping bag and a pot which served as a commode completed the furnishing. As I watched her hunched over the fire, draped in a blanket, hair bedraggled, eyes red with sleeplessness, a sympathetic greeting formed in my mind but came out differently from my mouth.

"Who's the odd sod now?" I said, restraining my tongue which was tempting me to more indelicate utterance.

"Where's the cat?" she asked, looking up at us standing at the entrance to her tent but screwing her eyes as if to see beyond us.

"Have you eaten? You're a picture of starvation. I brought you a cake."

"Where's the cat?" she asked again, this time with more urgency.

"The bus wouldn't take her, we had to leave her behind," I lied.

"Still wearing my Egyptian medallion, is she?"

"Oh, she'll wear it forever," I lied again, for as soon as I learnt of Eileen's protest I had unfastened the cat's collar and given it to Om who wanted to hang it on the Christmas tree, taken as he was by its bell and shiny medallion.

"Make sure she keeps it on, otherwise bad luck will befall us."

"I promise I will," I said, knowing that lying a third time would be my undoing, like the cock that crowed for Christ but had its neck wrung soon after, its body defeathered and put to pot.

"Have you not brought a spoon and plate?" she asked, unwrapping the cake. "How do you expect me to eat it?"

I looked at the dereliction of her tent, the soiled bedding, the urinal pot, the scattered lumps of coal, but she pre-empted my response.

"We have to maintain standards, whatever condition we find ourselves in." In the formality of her address I recognised Eileen the teacher. She was no longer in the decorous jacket and skirt she wore to school, no longer with a book in her hand, but still every inch the teacher.

"Standards, Molly, they're easy to uphold. A spoon, a plate, a resolution of mind. You smell urine in my tent, you see mess and madness, and you're betrayed by your senses, you surrender, you retreat back to the mediocrity of domestic habit. You abandon the nobility of the cause for the kitchen sink, the swept floor, the pruned roses in the garden. Nobility, though, is of another order, an attitude of mind that only needs an occasional spoon and plate, an occasional napkin, to reveal its materiality. Humble outward symbols of the depth of the human spirit."

I shuffled my feet apologetically and felt all the more inadequate when Stick sighed in deep appreciation of Eileen philosophising.

"How are your school lessons?" she asked, addressing Carol in a kinder mood. Carol, hiding behind me, horrified by the hag that Eileen had become, mumbled an answer.

"Speak up child," Eileen ordered as she would in the classroom.

"We've just finished *The Merchant of Venice*, Miss."

"I hope Molly has told you all about the Jews. I bet she hasn't, the timid thing."

"We talked about how the Christians cheated Shylock, Miss, and about how the Nazis tried to kill off all the Jews."

She frowned disapprovingly at me as at a junior teacher.

"Shylock was a hook-nosed horror, a greedy thief who had what was coming to him, just like the German Jews."

"Eileen! How can you?"

She brushed aside my protest – more shock than protest – and launched into a tirade against the Jews, accusing them of infiltrating every nook and cranny of British society, the law, parliament, the media.

"They drag us into war, which they fund and profit from, taking from each side. Remember the Rothschilds who financed the Napoleonic wars?"

I mumbled my ignorance. The hut became her new classroom as she expatiated upon the dealings of the Rothschilds during the Battle of Waterloo which netted them a stupendous fortune. She looked the very picture of a snarling dog and I remembered with horror the Christian women of my youth cursing Leviticus and the Jews for killing one of their own. They had come alive to inhabit Eileen's body like a legion of spirits. Eileen maintained her status as a historian, citing dates, personalities, incidents, but the rage in her eroded her credibility. Even Stick was taken aback, for it was of liberal Muslim sap and had once reminded me of how the Prophet Mohammad had ordered the sheltering of Jews against their persecutors and how to this day Jews lived in Arab lands peacefully and securely (apart from in Palestine, which Stick would not elaborate upon for fear of losing its temper). Eileen was now exaggerating Stick's version of history, charging Zionists with murdering British soldiers and Palestinian civilians, clearing space to plant their religion like thorns in Arab land.

"If they prick us, do we not bleed?" She grimaced at us and poor Carol touched my sleeve for protection. She started up again, blaming the Jews for the Suez war and I could feel Stick twitching in my hand, inspired to violence.

"Stop it! Stop it!" I shouted, the sudden distress in my voice stilling Eileen and Stick. "I don't know any Jews but Harold, he was no different from the other pals except he was circumcised and he was kind to me, he gave me money to set up a bank account…"

Eileen looked blankly at me but Carol, who must have intuited the indelicacies of my past, slipped her hand into mine and began to sob on my behalf. I hugged her to ease her crying, and as I did so I was overwhelmed by the strength of motherhood. I could barely understand what had overcome me and was surprised by my new resolve. Up to that moment I was a self-pitying woman, enfeebled by abuse, dependent on my Stick for solace, but Carol's lament on my behalf relieved me of my sense of victimhood.

"You must end your nonsense Eileen, end your hysteria," I commanded, my voice seeming external to me, not belonging to me but addressing me instead of Eileen. I attacked the hut, bracing against the tarpaulin poles, which were the props of my own past, and when the structure gave way and collapsed the whole of my body shivered with relief. It was not the savage cold which made me tremble but the realisation that my past was flimsy, make-shift, defective, and I could be free of it as easily as I could dismantle Eileen's hovel. I hauled her up from the seat, uprooting my pain, and when I kicked away the urinal and saucepan of coal I felt a mighty anger at the ways I had surrendered to the memory of the past. Even Stick was overpowered by my new temper, for I waved it against its will at Eileen, threatening to drag her back to the sanity of her home, if necessary by her hair.

"A right little raving Delilah, her, and you another Sampson the way you brought her house down," Stick said as we boarded the return bus. "Why are you lot so obsessed with the Bible, reliving all that violence as if unwilling to escape from history? Infidel as I am, you don't hear me carrying on about the Koran, about how–"

"Oh shut up," I snapped, stopping its prattle. The last thing I wanted to hear from Stick was a superior crowing. Eileen had exhausted me, resisting my mission to rescue her. She had pushed me away. I had toppled backward, falling on the ground, sliding about comically in an attempt to rise up. When Carol finally helped me to my feet I was covered in mud. I had felt the surge of victory over my past when I confronted Eileen but she had returned me to a state of uncleanliness. I looked at my muddy hands and darkened skin and suddenly remembered Om when he first appeared at my doorstep. My heart quickened at the memory, for Om, at first dreadful to behold, turned out to be a blessing in disguise, but more than the cliché, something more inexpressible, a winged angelic creature redolent of another world.

People in the bus glanced at me suspiciously as they had glanced at Om on the train to the gallery of Egyptian treasures. The passengers on the bus resembled those on the train. There was a mother clutching a young boy protectively. There was an elderly man so altered by the cold that the blood had drained from his face. It would not be in the least surprising if he keeled over and threw up in the final nausea of dying. I didn't bother to avoid their glances which spoke of unease, contempt, accusation.

Om opened the door but instead of acknowledging me as an image of himself went to hug Carol. Once more I envied Carol's youthfulness, the freedom with which she abandoned herself to his arms. The innocence of their relationship could not be extended to me. I lingered like a stranger at my own doorstep, then crossed over, reconciled to denial of self. The excesses of my past demanded abstinence now and for the rest of my life. I gripped my stick, wanting my hand to grow into its body and become an extension of its woodenness and inertia. Stick, though, tried to wriggle out of my grasp, refusing to accept its condition as a dead object.

"Oh ye abomination and incarnation of woe," Stick cursed. "Harken to their laughter which heralds the coming of a miracle and birth of such love that will usurp the thrones from which men strive cruelly to silence other men. Emperors of stupidity and of silence will be toppled, the world will echo to the cry of an infant who foresees the love and the agony of crucifixion."

I looked upon Om and Carol who were kneeling before the crib, laughing whenever their hands touched in the excitement of rearranging the bedding of straw, and Stick's utterance gave me new hope. Stick was a bridge between Muslim and Christian realms. I used to see Stick as a bridge between a living earth and my decrepit body, resenting the trinity, but it was converting me to a new creed. I rested it against the wall, walked up to Om and

Carol and knelt beside them, helping them to perfect the crib. Then, when it was done, by my own gladness and strength I raised myself, and as I did so I heard Stick moan, not in dejection, but in relief, for it was at last free from the burden of my wretchedness, free from the kingdoms of wretchedness which men had made of the world and my body. My hip would remain as incurable as the past, but no matter, for in this Christmas season I too would be reborn into a faith in the future. I was overcome with love for Stick. Ancient living forest had been silenced and hewn into ships of empire carrying slaves and plundered goods; into batons in the hands of warrior kings and their generals. Stick, stripped and chiselled into a servile instrument, resisted death as the notion and ambition of faithless men, and now, in me, he had found his first convert and disciple.

Eileen's fall was as complete as my ascent. She ranted about Jews to local and regional journalists covering her protest. Some papers depicted her variously as a monster of the same calibre of the Nuremburg war criminals. Others were less sensational, striving to understand how a perfectly respectable, tax-paying citizen, a model teacher and daughter, devoted to ailing parents, could have degenerated into a Jew-baiter and lover of Arabs. Some saw in her condition the disillusionment with empire, the end of Pax Britannica, understanding her to be a harbinger of the chaos which would overrun the colonies should they be granted independence. Others deemed her the future of the welfare programmes newly ushered in by a socialist government, welfare benefits threatening to create laziness, fraud, insubordination to authority, republicanism and a separation of Church from State. The odd sympathetic pamphlet appeared, linking her to a tradition of dissent and reformation, from Magna Carta through to Tom Paine and the suffragettes. Eileen, a teacher of history, was becoming a subject of history, though her notoriety was limited to Coventry and its immediate surroundings. I tried again and again to visit her, but policemen blocked my way. Coventry city council, at a special emergency meeting, had decided to cordon off the area around the munitions factory. My only contact with her was through the newspaper articles, each one making her less and less familiar to me as the quietly spoken, circumspect friend who used to take tea with me each Sunday. When my week's suspension from school was spent, my fellow teachers, knowing of our closeness, shunned me. Word of our friendship spread quickly, for when I appeared at the school gates a flock of parents parted, I passed through them as a pariah. Stick, though aghast at Eileen's behaviour, remained loyal to her, remembering our happy Sundays together. I faltered at the sudden silence which befell the staff room on my entrance. Stick was my constant reassurance.

"Silence is stupidity, remember? In their ignorance they shut up and want you to do the same."

Eileen was eventually shut up – in the Coventry jail, under charge of assaulting four policemen.

"Ridiculous!" Stick said, enraged by the illegality of it all. "How can a woman, small in stature, weakened by hunger, cause injuries to four hefty policemen? It's a stitch-up, literally, they're trying to stitch up her mouth!" And, learned as ever, it quoted to me the charter of the recently created United Nations: "Everyone has the right to freedom of expression and to impart ideas through any media and regardless of frontiers." We must go to her at once. I will counsel her on the laws of England and the civilised world pertaining to this matter. Even if the judge is a Jew he will be duty bound to release her. He cannot wield the cudgel of injustice over her."

Stick paused, remembering the many times it had raised itself over me in anger and accusation.

"Let bygones be bygones," I said to dispel its guilt. "We are in a new relationship, the two of us."

The national newspapers eventually gave coverage to the charges against Eileen when she was removed to London – for her own safety, the Coventry authorities claimed, fearing patriotic mobs would gather at the prison gates. Of course the truth was opposite, Coventry people's initial excitement in Eileen's case soon giving way to the daily routine of queuing outside shops for food (a full ten years after the war and many items were still in short supply), scrounging and petty thieving. Emergency regulations drawn up during the war prevented me from meeting Eileen, but I kept following her progress through the newspaper reports. In all our time of companionship she had never divulged significant details of her life, but now the London journalists, with large budgets for investigation, dug up the corpses of past misdeeds, revealing a character completely unbelievable to me. Shoplifting at the age of fourteen. Drunk and disorderly at nineteen in the company of communist subversives plotting mayhem. Five years spent in a commune in South London, the security services which infiltrated the group reporting on bread making, carpentry and pottery classes, political education, the printing of communist leaflets, unrestricted sexual relations. The security records were blank for several years, presumably because she had come to her senses and abandoned the profligacy of the commune. She reappeared in the files in the 1930s as a college student, then trainee teacher in Coventry. All surveillance of her ceased in 1937, the government no doubt convinced of her reformed character, or else having more dangerous radicals to pursue. The *London Standard* speculated that she had "gone underground" from 1937 onwards, a "Red under the Bed" leading a quiet conventional life but awaiting instruction from the enemy for revolutionary activity. The rival *London Chronicle* opined otherwise, presenting Eileen as a normal tearaway teenager, waylaid by communist plotters who debauched her mind and body, but eventually rescued by her devoted parents, returning to Coventry and to a respectable career. Her interest in matters Egyptian was entirely harmless, the newspaper claimed, appropriate for a teacher of ancient history, but this changed with a chance meeting in the British Museum with a Middle Eastern tourist, one El Kada who turned out to be a terrorist bent on blowing up the Houses of Parliament.

"What preposterous nonsense!" Stick said when I read aloud the story that El Kada had awakened Eileen's radical instincts and eventually become her secret lover.

"The *Chronicle* says they found receipts in various hotels around the British Museum proving the two of them overnighted regularly."

"Receipts my foot! Forgeries, that's all there is to it. You might as well believe in the Book of Mormon."

"It says El Kada is being held in a high security jail and he's confessed to recruiting Eileen."

"People will say anything under torture," Stick retorted.

"Torture? We don't do that here. We're British, remember?"

"Oh, I remember all right. I have centuries of memories stored in me. When I was a part of a tree in the Forest of Dean I witnessed deeds of torture and confession that the Devil himself would have ended. Poor chaps, tied to a tree trunk and slowly sliced up. They begged to confess, but the murderers still carried on–"

"Hush Stick, I don't want to hear!"

"Suffice to say that we are a nation of ancient expertise in engineering. We make glorious iron bridges and railway tracks. The thumbscrews too, racks, bridles, pinions."

"What can I do for Eileen, tell me?" I asked with sudden fright.

"Nothing. She's done for."

"But there must be somehow I can help, I can't just let her die in jail."

"She'll not die, she'll rot, and when the stench becomes unbearable they'll let her out."

I was on the verge of hysteria, but Stick remained callous.

"You'll get accustomed to her plight. I did. I grieved for the first victims, but so many came afterwards that I ceased to bother. Truth is, after a while, their screams became irritating, I wished they'd just die and leave me in peace."

Stick was resting against the sofa at my feet. I kicked it away in disgust.

"I used to have feelings but I'm a stick now, I've lost them, thank God. Kick me, trample, scorch, but you'll not get me to say anything but what I know to be the truth."

Stick, for all its egotism and declarations of wisdom, was wrong. Two weeks before Christmas and after a mere three days in custody, Eileen was released under condition that she took psychiatric treatment in a secure hospital. The magistrate dismissed all the newspaper accounts of treasonable behaviour as foolish inventions and condemned the police for wasting public money in prosecuting a woman whose only "crime" was defiance of government foreign policy. He ordered an investigation of the Coventry policemen who claimed to have been assaulted by Eileen, stopping short of calling them liars and perjurers. As to El Kada, another magistrate found him innocent of all charges. He was a tourist after all, and there had been liaison with Eileen but only of a sexual nature – "morally reprehensible in the eyes of many, but nevertheless an entirely *private* matter between two consenting adults. Allegations of a threat to public order and of high criminal intent are entirely unfounded," the magistrate said. Still, he ordered the Egyptian to be escorted to the airport and deported "for his own safety, given public sensitivities over the current conflict between our nations".

"She's free, she's free!' I announced jubilantly to Stick as soon as I read the news. "She'll be home for Christmas. We'll have a family reunion. Eileen will be aunt, I'll be mother, you'll be father, Carol and Om the children. We'll sing carols and give presents to each other and sit around a turkey wearing silly hats."

"There'll be nothing of the sort, believe me. Christmas will be the beginning of the end," Stick said dismissively.

"Don't be such a stick-in-the-mud, just because you're wrong doesn't mean I respect you less." Stick, however, continued to be grumpy and it was a relief when Carol came round to resume Christmas preparations with Om. Om was oblivious to the drama over Eileen, spending his time twisting, cutting and pasting pieces of old newspaper.

"Eileen's been let out, she'll soon be back with us," I told Carol, but she did not return my excitement. After her initial distress outside the munitions factory she never bothered to enquire about Eileen's fate. "Aren't you glad, aren't you looking forward to seeing her again?"

"Of course, Miss, she's a nice person," she replied blandly.

"Well at least Cat will show more emotion. Cat's the only one waiting for her to come home, it seems," I fretted.

"I'm not bothered, Miss, I knew all along she'd not be away for long."

"You did, did you? Well you were on your own, the whole country thought otherwise, but then they're not as clever as you." Arrogant brat, I thought, my disappointment in her stoked by her calmness and self-assurance.

"I thought the woman packing her suitcase to go away was her, but it's not," Carol said.

"It's not, is it? Who is it then?"

"I started to write my story again the day they arrested her, and as soon as I took up my pencil there was a kind of – kind of – a flash in my mind, and I saw another woman."

"So you had a moment of inspiration which equipped you to tell the innocent from the guilty, is that it?"

Carol ignored my cynicism, dwelling in the discovery which had come to her as she prepared to write. "It was just a flash but I knew it wasn't her."

"Who is it then?" I repeated, this time more anxiously, Carol's composure and lapse into serious contemplation making me wonder anew about her insightfulness.

"I don't know, Miss, there was a sudden light, but before I could look at the woman properly it went out. I only know it wasn't her."

"You must have caught a glimpse of her, even for a split second."

"I did, but I put out the light in my mind, I was scared. There she was, putting a man's things into a suitcase, and she was just about to raise her head to face me when I switched off the light."

"Leave her alone, Molly, you'll only upset her by carrying on," Stick urged and I ceased my interrogation, releasing Carol into Om's playful company.

It was Stick who proved to be prescient, not Carol, who never anticipated her parents' assault on me. It was on the Friday before Christmas week, the last day of the school term. The Christmas break would be a period of healing, a chance for the headmaster to forget, if not forgive, my insolence, and for my fellow teachers to start the year in a spirit of reconciliation. I put on a new pullover which I had bought as my Christmas treat but which I decided, impulsively, to wear on the last day. My face was ruddy, not from the frost, but from excitement at the prospect of teaching my class and sharing in their Christmas cheer. The ground was icy but I found myself not in the least clumsy, and felt that I could practically waltz through the school gates were it not for the people thronged there and the impropriety of behaving like a child. My frivolity of mind was terminated brutally. "Are you Miss Harris, our Carol's teacher?" a voice asked. A man separated from the body of parents and approached me.

"I am," I answered brightly, in my vanity thinking he was probably about to present me with a Christmas gift in gratitude for my inspiring work. He took his hand out of his jacket pocket and slapped me instead. I reeled back and slipped to the ground, falling heavily on my backside. Instinctively I reached out to retrieve Stick, but he kicked it away, leaving me a useless heap and figure of mockery to the parents. None of them offered to help or to chastise the man. They moved away, muttering as they left me behind with the bully. "Serves her right." "She had it coming to her." "Communist bitch." I was too much in a daze to take in their insults until an elderly woman parted from them, returned to me and spat into my face. "Nigger lover, shame on you!" Tears of outrage broke from me, I groped around for Stick, wanting to smash her ankles. "For the last time I warn you, leave me alone you ugly turd," I said, "and tell that Harold of yours he'll rot in hell with all the others."

"Harold? Who's Harold? You're barmy, that's what you are," she replied.

I must have appeared on the brink of some crazy act or outburst for there was trepidation in the way she hastened to join the departing crowd. "Give me a hand, you oaf," I said to Carol's father. He was so surprised by my boldness that he reached out and pulled me up. "Fancy you hitting a woman, and a cripple at that!" He blushed as he handed me my stick but the gesture of apology was short lived. Once more he squared up to me and put on a gruff masculine voice.

"You just be leaving our Carol alone, I'll not have her turning Turk or next time it'll be more than a slap!"

"Oh leave off man! You don't scare me, I've kept company with much worse than you." I wiped the tears from my eyes to look better at him. He was about my age, balding, with unhealthy skin, no doubt from years of cheap tobacco and beer. His jacket was second-hand, frayed at the cuffs and buttoned uncomfortably against his pot-belly. A typical working class man with a nondescript past and no future to speak of, except in the person of his talented daughter whose career one day could possibly redeem him from his status as a nonentity. I saw my father in him and pitied his condition. "Go in peace, I've done quarreling with you," I wanted to tell him but instead found myself bewailing the smudges on my new pullover. "Look what you've done! You've ruined it and I only bought it last week with good money." He shuffled his feet, dug his hands into his pockets but they were as empty as usual. His sense of chronic poverty froze all expression in his face. But then he quickly recovered his pride, repeating his threat to do violence to me should Carol ever be caught again in my company outside of school hours. It was a last feeble attempt to assert male dominance but seeing that I was not cowed he walked away and left me alone.

Alone. Alone. Alone. I beat the word out with my Stick as I returned home. It would not do for me to appear in class in soiled clothing. My absence, and news of the incident, would almost certainly lead to my dismissal. I would miss the children, dull as they were. I would miss their puzzlement as they stared at Shakespeare's words, their yawning, their outrageously stupid responses to my questions about plot and character. Their parents would shun me in the streets, I would grow to long for their presence, even if laden with insults. As to Carol, I could barely bring myself to contemplate her absence. Eileen's incarceration grieved me but the loss of Carol would be unbearable. "The beginning of the end, that's what you said," I sighed, but Stick was silent, brooding over the injury done to the two of us at the school gates.

The stench of excrement greeted me when I opened the door. "Om's in trouble, he's sick," I thought. As I hurried into the parlour my feet squashed something soft in the passage way. I steadied myself on Stick for the sight of faeces oozing out of a

142

parcel of Christmas paper made me want to bend over and retch. I unfastened my shoes and flung them aside. Om was in his usual place on the sofa, quaking, giving off an odious smell. I went up to embrace him, pitying his distress, but he flinched from me. Stick took command of the situation, speaking urgently to Om, who obeyed instantly, ceased trembling and started to babble.

"The bastards!" Stick bellowed. "I'll beat them all to a pulp, the bastards."

"Who, Stick? Who's done this to us?" I asked, begging Stick to speak calmly to me.

"Om said that as soon as we left this morning there was a noise at the door, a rattling and banging as if someone wanted to break in. He went to look, when a hand shoved a parcel through the letterbox."

I was aghast. In all my years in Coventry no one had shown me such contempt. The neighbours, the shopkeepers, the school teachers, all had looked upon me oddly, deeming me a solitary and eccentric woman. My gender and dependence on a stick, however, stopped them from any such active malice: shoving excrement through my letterbox wrapped up in Christmas paper. Not so much a present as a presentiment, for Stick warned of more to come.

"Bolt the door, draw the curtains," it commanded. But my horror had turned into sheer anger.

"I'll do none of the sort. I'll face up to them and show them to be cowards."

I turned to go to the door, to open it and proclaim my rage, but Stick blocked my path. "Om's clutching something, you better take a look." Stick spoke to Om who opened his hand to reveal the Egyptian medallion which Eileen had given for the Cat's collar. Stick could barely contain its emotion. "They've killed Cat, they put her in a bag and drowned her in the canal,"

Stick said. I pressed my hands to my ears but Cat's cries pierced my defences and Stick persisted in telling me the truth.

"No, no, no, they wouldn't have killed our Cat," I protested.

"Take control of yourself woman, this is an emergency." The word only served to bring on hysteria, spooling me back to my past. Emergency war regulations. Emergency rations. Makeshift emergency ambulances to ferry the wounded to hospital. Makeshift emergency hearses to ferry the dead to the churchyards. Stick urged me to stay calm but I couldn't until I looked at Om, who was withdrawn into himself, confused by my grief, wanting Cat and Carol to console him. My distress gave way to pity for him. He smelt as if he had just emerged from a pig-sty. "Go and bath yourself," I said. He didn't hear and I wasn't sure I had spoken. "What are we to do, Stick? I will not lock my door and hide away in the dark. They put Cat into a bag and drowned her in darkness. But we must fight the dark."

"It's a clash of civilisations and we're caught up in it," Stick said with such gravitas that I was brought to the verge of laughter. Horror, hysteria, weeping, and now an overpowering sense of the absurdity of the morning's events, and all events of my life. "I'm only a woman with a bad hip, bad sex, a missing cat, a friend in the mad-house, a schoolgirl writing a story which I can no longer follow, and a talking walking stick. Much much better and worse has happened to others," I said. This simple summary of my life suddenly comforted me and I felt that from that moment I would never again cry, never again succumb to victimhood. I had felt such a transformation before, when I had risen from the crib by my own gladness and strength. I had since lapsed back into helplessness, but now Stick's ridiculous talk of a clash of civilisations restored to me a sense of my ordinariness. Now I longed not for the miracle of change but for this condition of ordinariness alone. I was an ordinary person. My experiences, however cruel and disgusting, were still ordinary, for cruelty and disgust were matters of fact. I had risen from that crib with some vague faith in the future. Now I realised that loss – acceptance of loss, expectation of loss – was faith in the future.

Loss. Painful to imagine, but no amount of mental rehearsal can prepare you for its actuality, the regret, emptiness, helplessness. When the police came to remove Om, faith in the future seemed a set of hollow words; words fashioned in foolishness and self-deception. Some malicious person or persons had reported me for harbouring an illegal immigrant.

"We have reason to believe he stowed away in a boat bringing timber for the new Cathedral," the police said.

"I suspected so. Carol guessed as much."

"Carol? What's her surname?"

"She's only a schoolgirl, I'm the only one responsible for keeping Om."

"You do realise it's a serious offence to aid and abet an illegal immigrant."

"I didn't, officer. He appeared at my doorstep one cold night. I let him in like a good Christian. He's harmless, you'd do the same."

"Madam, this country will soon be overrun by coloureds. They'll threaten our way of life. They're an idle lot, scroungers, pickpockets, beggars."

"No different from folk around here then," I said.

"It's sympathisers like you who encourage the increase of coons in our country. You're a friend of Eileen Wilson, aren't you?"

"I am and very proud of it," I said, my defiance masking my anguish over Om's imminent departure. "Stick, explain to Om what's going on. Tell him that whatever happens we'll not abandon him. Tell him that police in our country treat strangers kindly, he's not to worry." The policemen leant away from me as I talked to my stick, obvious amusement on their faces. "It's

145

alright, I'm batty that way. Surely your secret file on me would have told you that."

They handcuffed Om and drove him to the police station. They took the crib with them and some decorations from the Christmas tree. Om had adorned it with paper birds and animals, their plumage and shapes alien to our native species. There were the usual angel and bulbs speckled with artificial snow which were Carol's contribution. I loved their muddled effort, Demerara wildlife nesting in our homegrown tree.

"Why do you need to take them away? For pity's sake, leave something for me to remember him by."

"Forensics," they said, dismissing me, dumping crib and decorations in the boot. So much for the season of goodwill to all men, so much for the forgiveness that the plans for the new Cathedral proclaimed to the world.

"Forensics! You'd think Om was a murderer or child molester," Stick said, mocking the excessiveness of the police. I wasn't listening, staring at the tree stripped of Om's queer and exotic handiwork.

"For a moment I thought I was special, but now Om's gone I know I'm just a nobody," I said.

"Don't start! One moment you're craving to be transfigured, the next you want to remain ordinary. And stop weeping, I'm fed up with you drooling all the time. Pull yourself together and put on your thinking hat. We have to act, not act up."

"I loved him, and all of us, truly," I blubbered. "Om's gone, the crib's gone, there's no God, there's nothing. Leave me alone to cry."

PART 4

1ˢᵗ January 1957

My dear Carol,

You will know by now, if you didn't beforehand, that I am the old lady in your story packing her suitcase. I put in my father's belongings and the clothes you and I bought for Om, though they are winter garments, quite inappropriate for Demerara, and the statuette of the Virgin Mary. Think of my suitcase as the Prince of Morocco's casket, but full of things strange and fascinating to the people here. Anyway, persist with your story and make of me what you will, marvellous, tedious, emotional, dull, whatever your imagination gives birth to. But don't make me daft, which no doubt is what people in Coventry are saying for following Om to Demerara. They deported him a few days after his arrest, offering him no lawyer or other counsel. When I called Coventry station to inquire after Om, the policeman told me this in a tone of triumph and before I could protest he put the phone down. I called the London newspaper but the receptionist refused to put me through to the news desk. I wanted to write a letter drawing attention to the slyness and injustice of his deportation, but when I explained this to the receptionist she too cut me off. I sat on the side of the sofa Om usually sat on and stared at the absent space of the crib and the empty shape of you kneeling beside it, your hands weaving straw or twisting wire, your face red with excitement, and Om affected by you, wanting to make strange and beautiful decorations to inspire you. I didn't light a fire. I just wanted to sit alone in the cold and dark. Then a miracle happened. I looked up at the cabinet where I placed the Virgin Mary out of Cat's way, on the top shelf. The statuette was glowing like one of those novelty toys with a bulb in it. Except there was no bulb, the Virgin's skin was radiant by itself, like a figure summoned up by a séance. I clutched Stick out of fright for it had been years since I had battled with the dead. I had lost touch with them and reverted back to a state of fright at anything out of the ordinary. The Virgin spoke to me, pacified me, told me to follow Om. The Virgin told me not to fear the foreign, that she herself was widely travelled, appearing in India, Nigeria, Gibraltar; she'd been all over the British Empire. So there and then I decided to leave England, to renew my life overseas. Harold tried to stop me. A shrivelled old woman was behind the desk at the travel agency and spoke to me in Harold's voice, saying that all the flights to Demerara were booked for months in advance and that in any case the cost would run into a few thousand pounds, much more than he had originally given me to put in the bank. He was lying. I went straight to the London airport and bought a ticket right away, cheaply, for the plane was half empty in Christmas week. I think too they took pity on me for I told them I was going in search of my son lost in the Demerara jungle. Harold still pursued me. When the plane was taking off and I looked out of the window there he was sitting on the wing, his jacket and trouser pockets stuffed with coins, ballast to keep him from falling off. I raised my stick at him and swore. He grinned at me. I must have been in a right state for the stewardess unbuckled herself and came to me, thinking I was a nervous passenger. I pointed out of the window but she couldn't see Harold. She pulled the blind down, hoping this would calm me. I held my breath as we ascended, and the plane shook as if Harold was trying to bring it down. The plane steadied, I raised the blind and there was Harold settled malevolently on the wing. But then the plane entered clouds, for an eternity it seemed, and when it emerged Harold was gone. The clouds had knocked him off. Such a feeling of freedom came over me that I shivered, the stewardess brought me a blanket and a cup of tea, bless her. All this sounds daft and perhaps it is in truth: when you read my journal you'll make your own mind up. Yes, I intend to keep a journal whilst I'm here, about my past and present, as well as writing letters to you. I'll have to find a way to get them to you, there is no post office here. They'll get to you somehow, or else you can just read my mind however far away you are. You're gifted that way – though some would call it a curse. Otherwise I will wrap the papers in a waterproof bundle, place them in a Moses-basket and into the river which leads to the ocean and you. Or I will fling them into the air, they will sprout wings and fly to you as Om came to me in Coventry.

*

Dear Carol,

Finding Om in Guiana was easy. A taxi ride from my hotel to the police headquarters, through the spacious avenues of Georgetown – a city of canals but much more picturesque than Coventry's, and stupendous wooden architecture, the most graceful and natural buildings I've ever seen. The police officer had him recorded in his book of deportees, at the top of the page, the only Guianese to return from England in December. The police officer remembered him well, for not only was he Amerindian – a people who rarely travelled far from their birthplace – but he had arrived home in style, in an aeroplane, not on the usual banana boat. "He must have been special to get such treatment, they usually come back ragged and half starved and out of their minds because of being chained in a dark cell deep below deck." He's special all right, I told the officer, but when pressed I had nothing to divulge, not really knowing what was special about Om. I found out his true name, Apotu, which is the name of his village – apparently none of the inhabitants have names except that of the village. The officer said he didn't know the meaning of the word but Stick told me afterwards it was a word without meaning. It signified everywhere and nowhere, everything and nothing, so it had no meaning.

I spent only one night in a Georgetown hotel, wanting to set off to the village as soon as possible. The hotel manager, a white man, said Georgetown had no museums or galleries, nothing to attract a tourist. There was a gift-shop somewhere in the city, selling bottles, bits of weaponry and coins washed up on riverbanks, mostly Dutch things of the eighteenth and nineteenth centuries. The manager told me that the rivers were scenes of great battles between the Dutch and the British, the riverbeds were strewn with the remains of sunken ships. Most of the history of Guiana is underwater, he said, and I thought of how Om had spoken of his ancestors living at the bottom of the river. I imagined their paths choked by pieces of ship's timber, and colonial litter. They cleansed their space of the rubble, throwing bottles, coins, guns, to currents which took them to the riverbank. I found myself wondering what Om's ancestors did to the white bodies drifting down upon them. Perhaps the crocodiles took care of these before they reached the riverbed.

The hotel manager kindly found me a boatman. Eileen once told me her brother had run away from Coventry and I must say I was startled by the manager's resemblance to her. He had the same coarse brown hair, the same blunt nose and morsel of a mouth but there was more to it than the physical, for there was a melancholy about him as if he had lost something that could not be retrieved, or sought something that could not be lost. I knew before coming here that Guiana had always been, since its discovery in Elizabethan times, a refuge for British runaways, people fleeing debt or imprisonment or some unspeakable shame; or else like Raleigh, chasing an impossible dream and fortune. I suppose being here myself makes me one of them, and all of them. I was tempted to ask the hotel manager what his story was, how he ended up in this most distant outpost of empire, but any revelation of his connection to Eileen would have unnerved me, so I kept quiet. I'm manic enough as it is. Stick keeps reminding me of my instability, cautioning me not to topple into total insanity. Besides, my quest was different, to find Om. The boatman had to be bribed heavily, muttering something about disease. It was only after the hotel manager barked at him and I weighed his pockets with money that he set off.

It took nearly twelve hours to reach Apotu. We left at dawn, the engine chugged and sputtered and smoked and cut off and started again, but I was not in the least impatient. When you are on the Demerara river, time and the absence of time are the same, a marriage such as I could never have imagined, the union of the vast stretch of water to the unending sky, with the native birds – spoonbills, cormorants, cranes – soaring and diving like drunken celebrants and wedding guests. None of this you can understand until you are on the river, which is spread seven, eight miles from bank to bank, its size all the more stupendous because of its emptiness. We were, for many hours, the only boat on the river, and when we encountered others they were but sporadic canoes at a far distance, each occupied by a solitary fisherman. At first the noise of the engine comforted me with its familiarity, reminding me of the motor cars and buses in Coventry, but I soon lost myself in the nature of the jungle. Trees line both banks for as far as the eye can see, an unbroken line which the hugeness of the river dwarfs, for mora and mahogany which tower to the skies, a hundred or more feet high, are, viewed from the middle of the river, like low hedges in the English countryside. It is only when the boat, seeking a safe passage through the currents, moves towards the river bank, that the comparison with England is shattered, the drunkenness of the jungle revealed, the columns of trees, the cat's cradle of vines and creepers, the crush of climbing plants. Near the riverbank the water is richly dark, converted into wine by some alchemy of soil and stone and leaf and bark. The jungle drinks it in, loses its senses, all is mayhem.

We reached Apotu just before sunset. I cannot tell how the natives learned of my coming but as the boat slipped ashore a huge cry arose from the crowd gathered to meet me. The women were nude, wearing scanty loincloths, their breasts and bellies exposed to view. The men too. The children were completely naked. But I soon recovered from the shock of their lack of clothing and was instead taken by the bead necklaces worn by the women and the feathered headdresses of the men. There was a musical ensemble, five or six men playing flutes (which I found out later were made from the shin bones of deer), others beating drums, each adorned with necklaces (the polished teeth of bush hogs, I was to learn). It was a simple ceremony, when I stepped on land (aided by a gaggle of excited women) I was garlanded with flowers and offered a gourd of liquor which I accepted too readily, for within a few minutes it took effect. The liquor, in my exhaustion from the day's travel (the sun had sapped my strength without me noticing, entranced as I was by the novelty of the landscape), made me unsteady. Luckily the same women who helped me off the boat came to my rescue, supporting me as they led me to a hut which was to be my private hotel. In my dazed state I called out Om's name, but the women hushed me as they laid me to rest in a hammock. "Oh dear, I'm such a nuisance, aren't I? I'm sorry to put you to such trouble," I heard myself saying, but my English manners were incomprehensible to them, the women merely smiling at me. I wanted to wash and get undressed but I had no energy left and fell asleep in the sweaty clothes I was wearing. A simple end to an otherwise unlikely day.

I woke up in a state of confusion and fright for the air was rent by screams of murder and torture. Innocent me, it was only the dawn chorus of parrots, nature's alarm which was to rouse me each morning thereafter. Om was standing over me. He lent towards me and whispered, "Ssh, ssh, ssh." I reached out to touch his face, but my strength had not returned and the liquor had not yet been neutralised. I fell asleep again and it was not until mid-afternoon (the same day, I think) that I stirred.

The hut was without door or walls but the natives had constructed a screen, made of reeds, at the far corner, where I could change without being observed. Two large pots of water were left beside the screen, the provision made for my cleansing. As for a toilet there was a raised wooden platform with an opening in the middle and at its base a trough which ran from the hut into a clump of trees. A special facility (no doubt at Om's request, he being influenced by the way we did things in England), for I was to learn that the natives performed their toilet under any convenient tree and covered over their traces with dead leaves and twigs.

It took me a while to get accustomed to these arrangements but I eventually managed, washing off my sweat and donning fresh clothes. I felt obliged to powder my face and put on some lipstick and eyelashes before stepping out to meet the natives, my English masking if you will. Om was squatting outside at a respectful distance, his back turned against the hut. When he spun round there was delight in his face and he gave off a smell of angelica. He was no longer tainted with the smell of beer. He called out and women emerged from their huts bearing food – grated coconut, pineapples, cassava bread – and gifts of clothing, though not in any material familiar to us in England. They were to show me later how they stripped the spikes of palm leaves,

153

boiled, dried and twisted the stripes into strings which were then spun to make hammocks, but in my case, being a stranger in need of cover, clothing. Rough on the skin and difficult to keep in shape but all the same a token of respect.

*

Dear Carol,

I'm glad to be here, glad, an odd word to use because I can't truly name what I feel. I spend my days just thinking: yes, thinking. My life has been so rapid that I've only *lived* experiences which have not been properly probed. Perhaps it is like this for all of us – we live always in advance of meaning for there is little time, outside of just *living*, for any understanding. So I'm slowing down so as to catch up with my life and to cache it in a private store where I can move the items about, juggle this against that, to try to glimpse some design. Perhaps there is none, but that in itself is a knowledge I would not have arrived at in Coventry for I never paused long enough to arrive, I was going on, going on, going on. Rambling and scrambling. So after two weeks of doing nothing, going nowhere, just collecting and recollecting random items, trying to find some kind of pattern, what have I discovered? What did Raleigh discover in Guiana and the thousands of explorers after him? I don't know but at least I am in the process of wanting to know. The everlasting life of the jungle is a strange comfort. I am gladdened that the flowers, the mora trees, everything that grows here will survive me, that long after I'm dead these beautiful (and dreadful) scenes will be as vivid as ever in the imagination of newcomers. At the same time the thought depresses me for I want to be eternal witness, or if not eternal I want to believe that my witnessing of them held some meaning. "Held some meaning" … for me, for the life of the place, for both? Why only "some"? And what "meaning"? I don't know, I am as yet a bog philosopher, but it is such joy to stop time, to reach back and retrieve something from the past, to hold it up in my mind and marvel at it as Raleigh would have done when he dreamt of discovering his first nugget of gold. In that instant Raleigh must have stopped being a man, never mind an Englishman, and become a new kind of creature as alien and unnameable to his old self as the jungle animals in his presence. But then he woke up empty-handed, woke up to the reality of Queen Elizabeth and King James and the gloom of a prison cell. Will I too wake up like this? No, I want to carry on not carrying on but arising from the past as a diver comes up from the bottom of the river with a pebble which, when chipped away, stripped by alchemical liquids, rubbed down with special clothes, reveals a diamond as blue as the iris of your eyes, Carol, yes, your eyes which so often looked at me in scorn, perceiving me to be a queer, lonely woman to be befriended only out of pity or only because I was the keeper of a treasure which was Om, whom I tried to hide from sight in the cache of my sole affection but whom you were determined – as determined as the greedy conquistador and adventurer – to steal from me, hence the slyness and stealth with which you penetrated my abode, made yourself at home in my sitting room, speaking nicely to me but all the time assessing the quality of Om like a Jew salivating at the precious stone in his weighing scale. I hate you Carol, I hate your spiteful youth, your story of a daft old woman packing her suitcase which you created just to offend me. I will never write to you again, I prefer to throw back the diamond into the river where it will quickly lose its sheen and become an ordinary stone again safe from your pubescent craving. Did I tell you that Harold was a Jew? Lazarus was his surname, he touched the opalescence in me and converted it into a currency of bright sores. Lazarus, Midas, Jews all.

*

Dear Carol,

I was shocked to read over my last letter to you, so much so that it's taken me a whole week before I could take up my pen again. Not because I was spiteful to you and lost my temper, for I know you will forgive me for the idiot-savant I am. And when you're older and in possession of the letter you will concede that there was a degree of truth in my accusation. No, what was shocking was my outburst against the Jews, which I thought Eileen had cured me of. A Jew never set sight on me, much less laid his mind on me. There was a man called Harold but I was never sure whether he was a Jew or merely rich. The last war shocked us, all those stories and pictures of starving Jews. Even the Salvation Army rattled collection tins for the survivors and though most of Accrington was hungry and suffering from shortages of everything from flour to paraffin we dropped in our coins religiously. But the stories kept coming, more and more dreadful, teeth pulled, gas ovens, cannibalism, too much, I started to dream of a concentration camp, a pen in which I was kept, a Jewess of your young age, and my father and our neighbours were my Germans, and did such things to me that when I woke I was too distressed to leave the house, I couldn't pass my neighbours on the street without marvelling at how I had transformed them into swine. I locked myself in, afraid of my imagination. My father worried over me, he thought me struck by some illness, a touch of madness inherited from my mother, so he let me be. Eventually I had to flee Accrington, my father packed me off to college in Leeds to train as a teacher. Up till then I was normal young lady in my mid-twenties and though my mother had recently died I was able to fill her place in terms of tending to my father. He was always sickly, I knew it was my duty to remain at home to care for him. Romance would come later, I was not impatient, for the meanest looking woman in Accrington was never short of a partner, and I was pretty, I turned a few heads though it sounds immodest of me to say so, plus I was schooled to the age of sixteen. But my father, frail as he was, insisted I go to college in Leeds to show my face to the world and recover my mind. I failed him for I could not escape from the pen, my role as a Jewess, and the men in college who I could have struck up a normal relationship with all became Gestapo, blond and menacing. I hid away again, and my father died soon afterwards. I tell you all this to explain why I loathe the Jew for she is myself, not even my shadow or twin. I sought darkened chambers and the snarling of dogs but Harold saved me, my father's dearest friend who gave me sufficient money to start anew in Coventry though I have spent all my years since blaming him for my condition. Now I am in Demerara, swamp or sanatorium I know not, but will bide my time and await whatever will befall me. Bless me in your prayers, and on the page when you come to write my life. My journal is fitful and unfinished, when you grow up you will compose from it a narrative. I write my history to warn you of men, warn you of my complicity in their doings. You will become a wordsmith, not like me, a wife to the unspeakable.

*

Dear Carol,

Weeks of lazing in my hammock, waking up or sleeping at any hour without the least care for time. The natives are not concerned by my lassitude. It is as if they expect me to rest after long journeying from another world, until I can get accustomed to my new surroundings. The women bring me food – fruit, cooked vegetables and goat's milk – and after I have eaten, a small calabash of a golden-coloured beverage which tastes like elderberry wine but which soon leaves me in pleasurable daze, so that the sunlight slanting across the roofs of the huts seems like a lavish coating of treacle and the birds which alight there are mired in it, struggling to take flight, their wings glued in the thick sweet substance of light. They grow exhausted, they cease their panicky cries and yield to the certainty of death, for snakes live in the thatched roofs, and I watch them emerge from their hiding places at their own leisure to take their pick of the birds. There is an utter self-assurance in the way they reach for the birds. Not with a jerky greedy lunging but with the deliberation, the elegant disdain of creatures accustomed to ageless ceremony and their practised role in it. Day after day I watch the snakes' performance, awed by their sedate motion, their brightly coloured heads like masks which secrete the nature of cruel appetite. I too become lulled by the inevitability of cruelty, which the masks transform into timeless ritual. The women bring me more golden liquor, preparing me for the day when I will arise from my hammock and venture fearlessly into the jungle, accepting whatever awaits me there. I drink from the calabash as from a sacramental cup and memory of Accrington recedes or else I envision my previous life differently, in a mood of forgiveness, for the appetite of the snakes is masked in the sacredness of ritual. I was a fledgling, a luscious novice, a virgin integral and necessary to the liturgy of sacrifice. This I come to believe, and my faith is deepened when night falls, the moon and stars laid out on an altar cloth like shimmering chalice and candle and sacramental plate.

Still, for all the acts of preparation I faltered at my first outing. Om woke me up with a breakfast of pineapples. He peeled the fruit, sliced it into cubes and offered it to me piece by piece. Satisfied that I was fed he left me to ready myself for the morning. I put on a dress of leaves and spun straw which the women had made for me and waited for his return.

He was naked but for a lap-cloth but he had painted his face white as if to reassure me of kinship. I reached for Stick but it wriggled in my hand, wanting me to be alone with Om. Since arriving in the country it had lost its boldness, content to remain lying on the ground of my hut gathering dust to disguise it from our wooded surroundings. "I too am overwhelmed by the jungle," I said, hoping to relieve its anxiety but the presence of so many alien trees must have traumatised it, confusing its sense of identity. It wriggled in my hand so I dropped the matter, dropped it onto the ground, and followed Om on unsteady feet. The jungle was on the outskirts of the village, beyond the cassava field which ended abruptly in a stretch of land once ploughed but now abandoned to bush. It was infested with weeds which gave out savagely coloured flowers, crimsons and dried-blood purples warning of the inhumaneness of the jungle before. Om strode ahead. The thistles snared my feet and the flowers suddenly reminded me of my mother's dress on the day she was killed. I turned back and sought refuge in my hut.

Om didn't express dismay or disappointment. He didn't even pause or call out to me. He disappeared into the jungle and an hour later returned with a handful of plums which he presented to me. Without warning he reached for my head and made me bow as he adorned me with a necklace of shining leather-coloured beads. He had obviously searched out the beads in the jungle. He lifted my head to admire his handiwork, his face lighting up in gladness. "Oh thank you Om," I blushed. "I'm really too old for presents, it would look better on Carol's neck."

Stick coughed, preparing itself for a jealous outburst. "The pagan has gone and married you, that's what he's done with that necklace. It's their way of signalling the conjugal, and a right sight you'll be stretched out under a coconut tree with Om on top of you and the whole village gathered to cheer. Do they know that you're barren? Best not to say, they might decide then you're only fit for the stewpot."

159

"There you go again, like spore blown away by a foul wind to create weeds in a flower garden. Why not be useful and do some translation for me?"

Om spoke, as if on cue and I looked to Stick for assistance. "Something about a white man, how they decorated him in a necklace when he died," Stick said at last, grudgingly.

"A white man in these parts? Ask him when and why."

Before Stick could speak Om reached for my hand and led me from the hut. I grabbed hold of Stick, and supported by the two of them entered the chaos of the jungle.

It was not the duskiness of the air which startled me – the roof of leaves a hundred and more feet above blocking out sunlight – but the blast of odours, like walking into a storehouse of perfumes except that the sweet scents drifting down from the flowers hung high, almost invisibly, above us, mingled with the stink of rotting matter and resin leaking from trees. It was this assortment of smells that Om had brought with him to England, of berries, feathers, dead insects, resin. I walked along the trail in a drugged state, the aroma of the jungle mingling with my sweat, petrifying it almost, weighing me down so that my movement was laboured. What a relief, after a half hour or so, to arrive at a waterfall. I sat on the rocks and the water tumbled upon me, washing me thoroughly. It was only a small opening in the trees, but the sun poured in as from a breached dam, so that when I sat away from the waterfall to dry myself my body was strangely lit. I looked at my arms and legs haloed as if belonging to someone singled out and blessed, and I remembered the first night with my father, the way the light had forced itself into my room, exposing me to his beak, a stone upturned exposing a gleaming white worm. I cupped my hand around that bird, believing it to be a fledgling fallen from its nest, but it was a crow crazed by hunger and would not relent until it was fed. "Take me back to my hut," I told Om. He understood without need of Stick's translation. I must have given off a spray of distress for he helped me to my feet immediately and returned me to the village.

That night a woman came into my hut and made a bed of branches on the ground. Om must have sent her to keep me company in case I remained troubled. I slept soundly though. When I woke up the next morning she had gone. Soon after I had dressed Om appeared with a platter of fruit. He watched me eat then fetched me a bowl of the golden liquor, thicker than usual, the texture of syrup. He waited for it to take effect. He said something to me which I seemed to understand, albeit fitfully. "Yes, I will follow you," I replied, the words coming from my mouth in his own language. He spoke again and I consented, picking up my stick and walking behind him towards the jungle. The liquor fermented in my mind, and by the time we reached the jungle arcade, past the cassava field, the clump of cashew trees, the thorny wasteground, I was almost fluent in native speech. As we walked through the jungle he paused to show me lives hidden to ordinary eyes and to name the trees and shrubs upon which they merged into invisibility. A piece of bark broke off and took flight, spreading wings to reveal a rusty-brown butterfly. A leaf fluttered down from the canopy but before it touched ground opened up into an olive mantis, showing off its filigreed body before disappearing into the greenery. We skirted around the pond but a jacanda crossed it effortlessly, seeming to walk on water, for its toes trod over lily-leaves. A small pile of vegetation beside the pond shifted to become a turtle, shaggy with loose skin along its neck. The dimness of the jungle gave way to light dropping from openings in the canopy, revealing wreaths of passion flower throwing themselves from tree to tree. It was a light too strong for human eyes; I stumbled with relief into the shadows, a temporary respite, for the light poured down again where trees had fallen from a storm and made space for the sun. Our passage was through a lattice of light and darkness so by the time we reached the waterfall I was in a daze, the water pounding on my head adding to my carefreeness.

Countless mornings afterwards, having drunk the fortified golden liquor, Om led me to the waterfall. My initial terror was gone, I spent hours bathing and drying myself on the warm rock. Stick's anxiety too gave way to rapture as it rested beside me in the midst of mora and eucalyptus trees. Accrington receded into an unreal silence, its noises drowned in the swirl of water. We listened instead to Om, hypnotised by his voice which rose above the sound of the water as if to becalm it. He told us of the history of his village – not history in the ordinary sense for time seemed marked by natural cataclysms. The first period was one of storms so fierce and continual that the fields could not be planted, the jungle around them grew sodden and died. Were it not for their ancestors who lived at the bottom of the river they would have perished. Nuts and berries fallen from trees upriver, beyond the reach of the storms, floated to the place where their ancestors lived and washed up on the shore. When the period of storms ended, disease set in, leprosy especially, but again the ancestors interceded, dredging up the river bottom for panacea in the form of leech-like worms which fed on pus and bad blood. The villagers survived but news of the disease spread to neighbouring tribes. The villagers were isolated, but without consequence. They grew their crops, they harvested the resources of the jungle, they worshipped their ancestors. The third period found them in a state of surfeit, the earth teeming with melons and cassava. It was only the coming of a white man which presaged calamity.

"A white man came? When?" I asked, this time alert to the anxiety in Om's voice. He had mentioned a white man before but the smells and noises of the jungle had dizzied my mind.

"There is no 'when' in these parts, remember? A white man came, that's all," Stick said, but I insisted on precision, suddenly irked by the chaos of the jungle.

Dear Carol,

I've been writing all my life so far, my mother, my father, all that has happened to me. Writing in spite of the drink they give me, which tries to brake my mind so I have to concentrate really hard and everything I recall is hard won and prized, though after I've written it down it appears so dreadful that I want to cast it away as you would something counterfeit. It's as if the jewels in the black Magus' coat which I showed you turned out to be worthless baubles and the whole nativity scene a fraud. Still, I continue to write for the very reason that when I read what I have written down everything appears unreal, nothing to do with me. It's not me, it's not my mother and father, all my life on paper belongs to someone else, some harpy and harridan (look up these words, try them out in your story, they're words with sweet melody). It's the drink they give me which makes me want to forget so that when I do remember it's shockingly bright, it's like my mind is a pool of electric eels. So bright that what I remember appears unreal, the eels lash out at each other and I grow crazy with light flashing in my eyes, like seeing stars which don't exist in truth but are particles of dust in my mind. Bauble, dust, fraud. This place is too much full of light. The flowers are too colourful, the leaves too gleaming, the toucans and parrots excessive as if some mad painter created the universe. I long for the grey skies of Coventry, the pavements, the concrete. If I stay too long here I'll want to lay waste to the place or prune it back.

*

Dear Carol,

There was someone here before me. Another white person, a man. I keep pestering Om but he'll not say. Or he's on the brink of saying when some terror stops his mouth. I can't think about how to entice him to talk about the white man. I don't have your saucy air and young breasts, I have to make do with threats. I've threatened to leave if Om doesn't tell me, take my sorry self back to Coventry. Why am I here anyway? I think it has to do with the white man. I must know, soon. I'm jealous of his coming before me. I hoped I was unique, that the natives had never seen a white body before and eventually might even worship me. I fancy being a deity. I miss being adored, handled preciously. But the white man has spoiled all that. He braved the legend of disease and landed in this place, breaching the history of isolation. I who have arrived after, probably no longer hold allure and mystery. I am common as muck. But no, they treat me with much kindness, bordering even on reverence. Yesterday the women brought me a rich broth. I was in a low mood and the food quickened my spirit. They stood around whilst I supped. My gratitude changed to suspicion. Am I being prepared, fattened up, for some slaughter? Today I refused all food but drank the golden syrup for it helps me to write lives that are not my own, though they purport to be me. The children come to stare at me. They watch my pen scratching out words, enthralled. I show them my father's things to maintain their excitement. They handle his pipe, cap and belt with trepidation and awe. These ordinary horrible things are transformed by their possession and gaze, they no longer belong to my father just as I no longer belong to him.

"I will not belong to you," I shout at Om, tearing off the necklace he made me a few weeks ago. "It's a chain you put round my neck but I'll not be your willing slave, nor will I surrender to the charms of the women who are preparing me for some black ceremony!" Om looks sadly at the beads scattered at his feet. "Come, Stick, let us be gone. Tell him to prepare a boat and a crew to paddle us back to Georgetown."

Stick will not budge. The jungle has reclaimed it. Stick is in love with the vegetation. It has gone native. Whenever I take up pen to write my memoirs it hops off to a tree at one corner of the village, a sarmoon tree, slender of trunk, with feathery branches which catch the breeze delicately, its pink flowers issuing a subtle perfume. Stick leans against the tree trunk like a love-sick suitor in a Shakespeare play.

"It is time, I tell you," Om says, not wanting me to leave him. He grasps my hand so resolutely that I have no choice but to follow him to a path of reeds by the riverbank. He stoops, removes a large flat stone, then another, and a third, retrieves a parcel and offers it to me. I peel off several layers of cloth – thinly woven but waterproof like the lap-aprons they wear – to discover a scrap of newspaper. It takes me some time holding the clipping at various angles to the light, before I realise that the faded photograph on it is of Coventry Cathedral, the old cathedral, its spires not yet blasted by German bombs. Instinctively I let the paper drop from my hand. A wind catches it, wafts it into the river. The current swiftly swallows and carries it away.

✻

Dear Carol,
I have been depressed for the past week so I've not written, my journal halted, and my letters to you. I go by myself to the waterfall and I bathe for hours until my skin is crinkled and yet I remain the same, no matter how hard I scrub myself with cara brush which the natives here use for soap. Thank God for the gourds of liquor but even that wears out faster than before, returning me too soon to my senses. The women increase its thickness to a treacle – out of pity for me – to prolong my intoxication. I wake up to a vision of myself as stained enamel, my father's pawned bath, taken away by the rag-and-bone man on his cart.

✻

Dear Carol,
I still cannot lift myself from the gloom brought on from Om's confession. A white man preceded me to this place. They killed

him, fed him to their ancestors who live at the bottom of the river by way of thanksgiving for all the sustenance given to them in eras of flood and famine. The scales have fallen from my eyes, I see them for the savages they are. My life is in danger but Om ignores my demand for a boat to take me to Georgetown and Stick is conspiring with him to keep me prisoner here.

*

Dear Carol,

More of the truth came out today. The white man was a missionary based at Coventry Cathedral. He must have been a man of courage to choose this place as his vocation. I pieced together Om's stuttering to discover that he was a kindly man. They shunned him at first, frightened by the sight of his colour, but the sun soon darkened his skin and he even learnt some of their language without benefit of the golden liquor which he shunned. To begin with he slept at the edge of the village in a canvas tent he had brought with him but the rain and sludge made a mockery of his dwelling. They invited him into the village, built him a hut, and made provision of food. They showed him the qualities of the place, the fresh springs, the spots where the ground suddenly gave way to snake-pits, and other secrets of the jungle. They taught him to name the fruit they planted by day and the night stars they looked up at. He spent most of his time reading as I now do writing. The villagers' initial anxiety waned, the white man was no longer an oddity. They went about their sowing and reaping, unaware of his gaze. It was only when he began preaching to them that his presence became troublesome. His pidgin language – a mixture of theirs and his – was barely comprehensible. He would grow frustrated at their blank looks and lack of response. All the same they listened, out of a politeness (or passivity) that was inbred in their race. He held up his book – obviously the Bible, but they were not to know, never before having seen a book. He read from it. He waved it over them. His voice was stern and sugary in turns. Their confusion turned to fright. Om stopped him. When Om told me this I no longer wanted to hear the rest of the story. It was Stick who steadied me, urging Om to continue. Stick insisted on interpreting Om's tale.

"Never before had there been a killing in the village, neither of human nor animal. That's why they are vegetarians, they just have no concept of killing."

"So how come Om murdered the missionary?" I asked in disbelief, accusing Stick of lying to me, of being enamoured of the place and wanting to excuse its cruelty.

"It was not murder. People here don't know how to murder. One day Om picked up a stone and flung it at the man's head. As simple as that: a stone travelled through air and stopped at his skull. Result: death. Stone, air, skull, death. Om didn't understand it, no one did, but all knew that something original had happened in their midst. Think of when the wise men first bent over the crib and caught sight of Christ – the same awe and anguish."

*

Dear Carol,

Stick weaves me a tale so fantastical that I doubt, I retreat to the waterfall to cleanse myself of hallucination, but on the way there I pass a clump of trees which have burst into blossom, dense masses of white flowers nestling along each branch so that the trees appear weighed down with snow. A wintry landscape in the midst of the jungle which makes me shiver instinctively. At the base of the trees are anthills built of yellow clay, resembling summer haycocks in an English field. I return to listen to Stick, for everything in this place is fantastical.

Om speaks through Stick of the shock of the new, death by a human act. I ask Stick "did Om intend to kill?" and Stick says the question makes no sense, neither then nor now. "It happened. They took the body to the riverside and lowered it in, hoping their ancestors would fathom the mystery of the event. The body floated off and disappeared, and they went back to tending their fields, but for all their attempt at calmness a fear of retribution surfaced. For the first time in their history they began to doubt whether the effects of what Om did – what they all did, since Om was all of them – could be withstood by their ancestors. Perhaps the stranger would spread disease amongst their ancestors, the malady which had lain dormant in the land leaching into the river and killing their ancestors a second time; the body of the missionary a diseased bridge between earth and water. Who would then protect the villagers should flood and drought return? And would other strangers come searching for the missionary? They decided to end all trace of him, burning his clothing and eating his Bible. Eating it, for he had held the book aloft and spoken from it, words coming from his belly and mouth. Burning the Bible would not do, it had to be returned into the body, so each villager was fed pages. A little way into tearing off the pages one by one they came upon a newspaper photograph of Coventry Cathedral which the missionary had folded and inserted into the Bible as a bookmark. The villagers looked to Om for guidance. For some inexplicable reason Om decided that the photograph should not be eaten, nor should it be burned, but instead buried on the riverbank, close enough to the missionary and the ancestors, weighed down with stones, a bridge of potential reconciliation between earth and water."

*

Dear Carol,
If I had my way I'd throw my stick into the river and let it sink and come to rest among the savages who apparently prosper at the bottom. Stick, though it is not ready for the underworld, has

rooted itself in the anthropology of the tribe on land in preparation for that eventual journey. Stick fills my head with stupidness, telling me that the tribe, having cannibalised the Bible and buried the photograph (which Stick speculates – no doubt to taunt me – was inserted as a bookmark in the middle of the Book of Leviticus) then sent Om to Coventry where he found me in error. That is what I am, Stick says, a mere error. "When someone dies before his time they can dream him back into life. It's normal practice for them. Om was charged with the dreaming, he was sent out of his body to roam abroad in search of the missionary, and return his spirit to Demerara, to be placed in the body of a newborn. Om got lost, poor thing, none of the tribe had ever had to dream beyond the boundaries of the river. Coventry was foreign land, like a moth stunned by moonlight he flew into your path and rested, and remained, for instead of sending him on his way you kept him prisoner. Eventually, having regained the strength, he dreamt himself back to Demerara, and you with him."

"Why me?" I insist against my will, not wanting to partake in Stick's fantasy yet repeating the question.

"Because you were kind to him, and the first thing his spirit saw when he entered your parlour was the statuette of the Virgin Mary. The missionary had an identical statuette. Perhaps Om thought that all white people were versions of the missionary, so you'd do as much as anybody else. None of his tribe had ever been on a mission to dream a white man, so the confusion is understandable."

"Is that why the children play with my father's possessions but shun the Virgin Mary? They run away when I try to give them the statuette."

"It reminds them of the time of trouble, when the missionary arrived, so they scoot."

"And is Om still in a dream state? Am I still part of his dreaming, is everything happening now unreal, you, me, the jungle, this conversation?" I press Stick again and again for an answer but it was resolute in its silence.

*

Dear Carol,
So there it is. I am an actress in some savage's dreaming mind, an item of fantasy. Nothing has changed since my time in Accrington. And there's nothing special about me, Om dreamt me by mistake. It is time I woke him up, cracked open his skull to make my escape.

"Well, you are not a complete accident, there is some method in him finding you," Stick said, but at first I would not be consoled. "No, no, I tell the truth," Stick insisted, assuring me that it had discoursed at length with Om on the matter and had concluded that dreaming was a sacred act, it permitted neither error nor deviation, though its effects may at first appear to be contrary. "There is some blinding logic in you being here," Stick said, and I was flattered into acquiescence, deciding to remain in the village a little longer.

*

Dear Carol,
Many days have passed since my discovery of the murder and I've settled back into life of the village. The women teach me to twist strings into the shape of cloth. They show me how to weave reeds into simple baskets. Animals are loved here even more than in England, ant-bears, monkeys, tapirs, come and go unmolested, people leave out food for them. Only when an animal dies do they make use of its bone, teeth or feathers for flutes, necklaces and headdresses as a way of commemorating its beauty in permanent art. I bathe in the waterfall or sit on the riverbank to watch egrets taking flight in a great surge of white or hummingbirds dipping their beaks in the hollow of flowers.

170

A life of idleness and bliss, but always a foreboding of... I don't know what, but there are moments in which I seem to wake up from Om's dreaming, then I am dragged down into sleep again, and in the split second intervals I glimpse Harold, Terence, Corinne. I seem to know that the missionary was Corinne's uncle, that she is coming to Demerara to continue his work. She will teach the tribe nutrition, the benefits of fish oil for brain activity and meat for muscle development among children. She will clothe their nakedness. They will worship her as Our Lady of Demerara. Terence is coming equipped with books. He will teach them irrigation, put them to work digging canals and clearing large areas of land of trees, so that they can diversify as well as increase their harvest, and trade profitably in Georgetown's markets. A shop will eventually be set up in the village offering goods brought from Georgetown – shoes, torches, and the like, but especially implements like metal forks, hoes and shovels to replace the bits of wood and stone lashed together with string which they use. Corinne and Terence will bring Joseph Countryman with them, they will cure him of his ailment by marrying him to a native woman. Joseph will replace straw huts with solid wood and slated roofs. Smithy will follow. He'll show the villagers how to make metal from molten rocks, which they can shape into spoons. No longer will they eat with naked fingers. Thank God Eileen is mad and shut away, otherwise she would come to make folk mark time. Altogether life in the village will be made more healthy, labour less arduous. These acts of charity are to be funded by Harold's family who have set up a trust in his memory for the relief of child poverty. I seem to know all this future as my mother used to know the past of Joseph Countryman and Caroline with her black pudding, all the people who lived in our house or used to own our crockery. This is why I have been brought to Demerara, to intuit the future so that I can bring salvation to the tribe.

I go to warn Om, at last becoming the prophet I longed to be. "Beware the end of your people and their ways. If you refuse to hearken unto me you shall be smitten before your enemies and the land shall not yield its increase and the river will be bloated with crocodiles. They're following me to Demerara, Terence and Corinne, you have to rid yourselves of them. I could try casting a spell, making them break out in a rash and retreat back to England in search of a cure for leprosy, but I failed before, I don't trust my power. I'm only a prophet, not the big Jehovah."

Om, lying in his hammock, eating cashews, ignores me altogether. It is as if I am of no presence. I shake the hammock but he will not budge. I raise my voice, to no avail. Om obviously can neither see nor hear me. "It's all in your mind," Stick says, but I accuse it of being itself a nutcase, besotted as it is with a living tree.

"You have to warn them," I urge Stick. "You have to use all the military knowledge of your Muslim forebears and show them how to make weaponry, powder that will explode, metal-tipped spears, whatever will repel the crusaders."

Stick will not heed my warmongering. "Om brought you to Demerara so you could recover from your madness and marauding pals. And what do you propose instead? You want to bring your civilisation to them, at the heart of which is war."

＊

Dear Carol,

You came at last to comfort me, early evening, the villagers dressed up in paint and feathers, sitting around a fire, holding hands, singing or making hideous cries. The moon was as black as Harold's eye-patch and beyond was the skull of space. We were all on the cusp of destruction, in spite of their vivid colours and

172

plumage. They called to their ancestors, they fed the flames with capara leaves which choked the air with smoke, and the sky cracked with lightening. The storm would drown us all and when it ebbed Terence would step forth from some ark, with Corinne and the rest in train, groom and bride and attendants in a new marriage with the earth, which Jehovah would bless, and they would multiply abundantly and wipe out all traces of Om and his tribe. But in the midst of my lamentation by the waters of Demerara, you came in the form of a bird, not Noah's dove with an olive leaf in its beak, but carrying a page, or rather, a morsel of page. You fell from the sky as if downed by lightening, into the fire of capara leaves, the villagers stopped their noises, the thunder ceased, the snakes in the rooftops slid away. I broke the silence, called out your name, you rose from the flame and flew to me and I cupped you in my hands, thinking you hurt, but you stopped my pity, opened your beak to show me paper which by miracle the fire had not even singed. I took it from you, stared at it, seeing nothing. There is nothing on it, I said, but you anticipated my grief. "I have not yet begun to write anew," you said.

"But what about your story of the old woman and her suitcase?" I asked.

"That was born of the troubled mind of a fledgling, I am no longer such a creature." You fluttered in my hands as if to show off your changed condition. I began to resent you again, remembering you as a saucy teenager, tormentor of men, but you stilled me with utterance of such seeming promise that I relented. A bright child you said your teachers deemed you, giving you extra lessons after school, as I was once offered. A prized scholarship to University followed, far from the moral and physical ruins of Coventry. In the 1960s, you said, women were free to exhibit giftedness and independence from men. You got a degree in English Literature. Appointment to the Royal

173

Shakespeare Company as a trainee director. Applause in the local and national newspapers as a precocious talent, which awed your parents, raising them to a pride beyond the lowered expectations of their Coventry upbringing, and money enough for them to move out to a modest but comfortable house in Warwick, close to the Shakespeare theatre. "And it was in the library of the theatre and in the seclusion of books that I began to compose your life," you said. "I imagined you as Portia, as Sycorax, as Lear's Fool, then I tore up all the pages and started again, writing you as a piece of Accrington abuse, but after a chapter or so I rid myself of that version of your history. I have come to you now for inspiration for I will conceive of you neither in the crucible of Renaissance drama nor in the furnaces of the north."

"Who am I then, tell me who I am," I cried.

"You are what I plot to become. I am twenty-five now and men have not yet turned me into swine, nor will I permit them to. I love them on stage, I direct their passions, I tutor them in the language and gestures of romance, but when the play is over I have my body to myself, protected by new medicines from the curse of childbirth, so I seek the sanctuary of the library in which to conceive you."

Silly girl, I thought to myself, yet still wondrous to want to mother me in new pages. I am nothing but a well-thumbed, broken-backed text, worms have hatched eggs in my spine and destroyed my standing. It will take a miracle of imagination to make me upright.

"What will you plot of me in your new age?" I asked, but before you could reply Om came up to us, delight inscribed on his face, for he recognised you. He tried to lift you out of my hands which were cupped in prayer and benediction. I shooed him away as a dangerous cat and flung you towards the heavens, watching you fly from me, banking at the river, following its path out to the sea, and then to England. Om too stared after you, his eyes wet with sorrow, wishing you safe passage. He smelt of fresh lime-juice, the ancient remedy of English sailors against scurvy. To think the common lime provided the chemistry for Empire and all its murderous achievements. I took pity on him. I explained that you were not to be touched by him, for he had killed, he had become an accidental Cain, and his habitation was cursed because he had brought me here in error. Soon there will be flood, then the earth seeded freshly by men made sturdy by lime. I explained that you, Carol, had no place here, nor he in England, except in the sanctuary of your imagination. Om listened without comprehension, as innocent of the future as he was of past error, and all the while his people sat around the fire, singing or wailing in feathered glory, calling upon ancestors who would not come to them, for only skulls lay at the bottom of the river: the bustle of the living was so much superstition.

"You were wrong to preach so bleakly to Om, you were only speaking out of your own emptiness," Stick said, not in its normal sneering way but with a conviction that suggested it possessed some hopeful knowledge hidden from me. I was curious as to the source of its faith, but a sudden weariness overcame me, I drifted into sleep, abandoning it to its folly, abandoning Om, the villagers and the Demerara jungle as figures in a demented landscape. A sound sleep, without a drop of golden liquor, will cure me of hysterical vision. I nestled in my bed of troolie branches dreaming of the ordinariness of England, doubting your projection of a future space transformed by women's assertiveness. 1960s England was a foreign world to which I could not return.

*

Dear Carol,
I can neither stay here, in a primitive culture on the cusp of change, nor return to England which has yet to recognise women

as equal to men. Om and his folk are too trusting, too peaceful, too welcoming, to resist the coming of the missionaries (who really ought to stay back in England, to change things there for the likes of me). But perhaps they will learn to hurl rocks as Om once did. In any case I don't want to stay to chronicle their future. As for the present England, what clemency is there for me? You appeared to me, talking of a changed future, but it was only in dream. Your presence though, real or not, did presage storm. Earlier today there was a sudden thunderclap, the rain came down with such clarity, such an outpouring as if there had been some accident in the sky and an enormous continuous spillage of light. Water swirled around the huts which appeared to be boulders in rapids but were in truth hollow eggshells easily smashed, washed away. The thunder clapped again and again, sounding like my father's voice. All the huts were wrecked and washed into the river. My own possessions, my suitcase of English clothing, my mementos of my father, my Virgin Mary, all were lost to the flooding, except my scribblings to you these past weeks. When the storm ceased the place looked as if it had been bombed. It is time for me to leave before I bring the villagers further apparitions of war. Om seems to understand this. Without me asking he has built me a dugout, more a crib than a canoe, for it can only hold one person and even then you have to curl up to fit in it. Om smelt of senna as he fashioned the vessel, for he is sick of heart at the prospect of my going.

I will wait for the tide. When the time is right I will climb in and pull over me the covers which Om has rigged to the sides. Curled up, covered from sight, I will float to wherever the currents take me. I will fall asleep and dream I am in my mother's womb, that when I wake I will be in the land of her promise, and in the alchemy of your imagination.

No-one but Stick comes to the riverside to bid me goodbye. It is speechless. So am I. There is too much love, too much grief between us for words. I am about to leave when Stick suddenly turns from me as if in cruelty, but it is only then that I see a tiny sprig issuing from a crevice in its body auguring mongrel leaf and bud and flower. The Demerara jungle has embraced Stick in a new kinship and adventure into life. A thousand years after I've turned to dust it will bear witness, as a living tree, to the love, to the grief, which stops us now from speaking words which have become needless.

The Macmillan Caribbean Writers Series

Series Editor: Jonathan Morley

Look out for other exciting titles from the region:

Crime thrillers:

Rum Justice   *Jolien Harmsen*

Fiction:

The Girl with the Golden Shoes: *Colin Channer*
The Roar of Shells: *Dara Wilkinson*
The Festival of San Joaquin: *Zee Edgell*
The Voices of Time: *Kenrick Mose*
She's Gone: *Kwame Dawes*
The Sound of Marching Feet: *Michael Anthony*
John Crow's Devil: *Marlon James*
This Body: *Tessa Mcwatt*
Walking: *Joanne Allong Haynes*
Trouble Tree: *John Hill Porter*
Power Game: *Perry Henzell*

Short Stories:

Catching Crab and Cascadura: *Cyril Dabydeen*
The Fear of Stones: *Kei Miller* (shortlisted for the 2007
   Commonwealth Writers' Prize)
Popo and Stories of Corbeau Alley: *Nellie Payne*

Poetry:

Poems of Martin Carter: *Stewart Brown And Ian Mcdonald*
   (eds.)
Selected Poems of Ian Mcdonald: *Edited By Edward Baugh*

Plays:

> Bellas Gate Boy (includes Audio CD) : *Trevor Rhone*
> Two Can Play: *Trevor Rhone*